**Trained toge~~ther~~ ~~a~~t ~~the~~ ~~academy~~, ~~these~~
six women w~~ould~~ ~~help~~ ~~each~~ ~~other~~ ~~in~~ ~~time~~ ~~of~~
need. N~~ow~~ ~~one~~ ~~of~~ ~~them~~ ~~has~~ ~~been~~
murdered, and it is up to them to find the
killer, before they become the next victims...**

Alex Forsythe:
This forensic scientist can uncover clues others fail to see.
PROOF by Justine Davis - *May 2005*

Darcy Allen Steele:
A master of disguise, Darcy can sneak into any crime scene.
ALIAS by Amy J Fetzer - *June 2005*

Tory Patton:
Used to uncovering scandals, this investigative reporter will get
to the bottom of any story—especially murder.
EXPOSED by Katherine Garbera - *July 2005*

Samantha St John:
Though she's the youngest, this lightning-fast secret agent can
take down men twice her size.
DOUBLE-CROSS by Meredith Fletcher - *August 2005*

Josie Lockworth:
A little danger won't stop this daredevil air force pilot from
uncovering the truth.
PURSUED by Catherine Mann - *September 2005*

Kayla Ryan:
This police lieutenant won't rest until the real killer is brought
to justice, even if it makes her the next target!
JUSTICE by Debra Webb - *October 2005*

ATHENA FORCE:
**They were the best, the brightest, the strongest—women
who shared a bond like no other...**

Available in July 2005 from Silhouette Sensation

Exposed
KATHERINE GARBERA

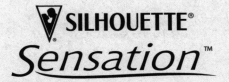

SILHOUETTE®
Sensation™

*First published in Great Britain 2005
Silhouette Books, Eton House, 18-24 Paradise Road,
Richmond, Surrey TW9 1SR*

© Harlequin Books S.A. 2004

*Special thanks and acknowledgement are given to Katherine Garbera
for her contribution to the ATHENA FORCE series.*

ISBN 0 373 51324 0

18-0705

*Printed and bound in Spain
by Litografia Rosés S.A., Barcelona*

KATHERINE GARBERA

is an award-winning, bestselling author for Silhouette. Katherine started making up stories for her own benefit when she was on a competitive swimming team at school. Though she went to the state championships and usually won, Katherine says her heart wasn't in swimming but rather in the stories she created as she swam laps at practice. Katherine holds a red belt in the martial art of Tae Kwon Do and vows that there's not a piece of plywood out there that can take her in a fair match.

Readers can visit her on the web at katherinegarbera.com

To my family—Courtney, my little kick-*ss girl who knows there's nothing she can't do. You make me so proud to be your mum! Lucas, my stubborn won't-give-up-until-I've-tried-every-avenue guy. And Matt, who gave me the greatest gift of all—our loving family.

Acknowledgements

Thanks to Shannon Butler, who took time out of her busy schedule to explain to me how the television news business works and how to conduct an interview with a man who'd come back from the dead.

Thanks to Amy Fetzer and Cathy Mann, who helped me with the military stuff.

Thanks to Sue Kearney for helping me out when I thought all hope was lost.

Thanks especially to Eve Gaddy for always being willing to listen.

Chapter 1

Victoria Patton held the phone away from her ear for a second and carefully covered the mouthpiece. "Hot damn!"

It looked as if all of her hard work had paid off. Of course, a good deal of luck was responsible for her being in the office when her boss had called in with the story. But he'd specifically asked for her, so she knew it was the break she'd been waiting for.

She pulled the phone back. "Of course, Tyson. I'll be ready to go by six o'clock."

Smiling, she hung up the phone, leaning back in her office chair. The halls of UBC, United Broadcasting Company, were quiet during the lunch hour. She spun her office chair around and stared out at the skyline of

Manhattan. An office with a nice view wasn't bad for a girl from a cattle ranch in south-central Florida. Days like today made the hard work and separation from her family worth it.

She turned back around and took in the evidence of how much she'd already achieved. One wall of her office held her journalism degree in a frame that her father had given her. The other wall held awards and framed photos that she'd picked up during her career. Her low credenza had neat and orderly shelves, but the top was cluttered with photos of her friends and family.

The surface of her desk held a blotter that she used to jot notes on and a green alligator pencil cup her brother had sent her when she'd done a story on the Florida Everglades. She also had a PVC figurine of Buttercup from the Power Puff Girls, because her practical joker co-workers thought she resembled the steely-eyed, tough-as-nails girl.

Tory was an up-and-coming television news reporter who'd been proving herself on the national level for the past five years. At five feet two inches tall, she knew she wasn't exactly an imposing figure, but her insightful questions and keen ability to read between the lines had given her an edge few reporters had. She had black hair and green eyes that she'd been told were as mysterious as a cat's. She knew that line had been corny flattery, but it suited her image of herself. At the age of twenty-eight, she was poised to take the national news media by storm, following in the footsteps of her role model, Diane Sawyer. At least, once she completed this interview she would be.

She was young to be considered for the job that her boss, Tyson Bedders, had just offered her—an exclusive interview with Commander Thomas King, a navy SEAL who'd been presumed dead for the past six months after a failed mission in the volatile island country of Puerto Isla in Central America.

Bedders had received a call from Joe Peterson, a public-affairs officer with the U.S. Navy, inviting Tory to go to Puerto Isla and interview King. Tory was to contact the minister of foreign affairs once she arrived on the island. The minister would coordinate the interview.

The details of King's mission were sketchy, but she knew that the members of the SEAL platoon he'd been directing had all been killed and King had been declared dead with the rest of the troop. According to the information Tyson had, King's platoon had been ambushed when they went in to rescue a group of American hostages being held on Puerto Isla.

The phone rang before she could completely digest the fact that she was leaving for Central America in less than six hours. There was a lot to do, including contacting her favorite cameraman, Jay Matthews. She wanted someone with her whom she could count on to film the story the way she wanted it captured.

"Patton."

"Hi."

It was Perry Jacobs, her boyfriend. She smiled to herself. Perry said he was too old to be anyone's *boy*friend. He always referred to himself as her significant other. She hated that term, because it suggested that there was nothing significant about her without that other.

Perry was a producer at UBC and they'd been working together for more than five years now. They'd been dating for the past four. He was nearly twenty years her senior and had more experience and knowledge of the business than anyone she knew.

Tory had been attracted to Perry from the first. At the start, she'd ignored the chemistry, not wanting to be fodder for the office rumor mill. Then they'd worked together on a feature story in Virginia, and the relationship had grown from there.

"Will you be home for dinner?" Perry had recently asked Tory to move in with him, and she still wasn't sure about the situation. Her relationship with Perry was one of the things in her life that she questioned.

Which was why she'd kept her own apartment and never stayed over with him more than once a week. She didn't want to encourage Perry to think too strongly in terms of permanency until she knew for sure that she really wanted to be with him for the man he was and not for the producer who had helped to make her into a top-rate journalist.

"Can't. I'm going to Central America on assignment."

"Where?" he asked. There was a note of resignation in his voice, and she suspected he knew that even without the assignment she wouldn't have come over tonight.

"Puerto Isla. Tyson got me an exclusive with a navy SEAL who'd been presumed dead."

"That sounds dangerous."

Perry was right. Puerto Isla *was* dangerous. The small island was still struggling to keep its new government in place after a bloody coup four months earlier.

Alejandro Del Torro, the new leader, had been cooperating with the U.S. government to get much-needed aid to his suffering people. He'd come to power after leading a rebel movement. The people of Puerto Isla were leery of following another military man, but Del Torro was only an interim leader and was organizing the government and preparing to hold elections within the next six months.

Before Del Torro, the island had been controlled by Diego Santiago, a dictator and suspected drug lord, a man who had allowed the island's coca-plant ranchers to supply many South American countries with the leaf that had become a part of their daily life. A leaf that the U.S. government was trying to eliminate because it was used to make cocaine and crack. Puerto Isla also served as a convenient stopover and refueling place for planes en route to Miami and the profitable American drug trade.

Tory was glad that she was fluent in Spanish. Languages came easily to her, and she figured she'd be able to communicate easily with the locals once she was on the island.

The interview was a step up from her usual kind of exposé assignment. Typically her stories involved going undercover with a hidden camera. Last year she'd been inside a women's maximum-security facility, which had been chilling and had given her nightmares. Tory suspected that any juvenile delinquent who spent one night in that facility would never commit a crime again.

"Tyson thinks I'm ready for it," she said. She'd like to hear that Perry did, too.

"Well, then I guess you are."

As a vote of confidence that one sucked. She shrugged it off. "I've got to get my stuff together. So I really can't talk."

"I understand. When will you be home?"

"I'm not sure. Probably three days." She opened her desk drawer and pulled out her passport and immunization record.

"Want a ride to the airport?" Perry asked.

"I think I'll cab it. Don't you have a story airing tonight?" Perry sometimes worked on Tory's stories but he had a stable of reporters that he produced.

"Yes, but I'd make time for you, Tory."

That warmed her heart. Moments like this one made it hard for her to decide what to do about Perry. "I know you would. Take care."

"Be careful," he said and hung up.

She dropped the phone back into the cradle and started making a list of things she had to do before she left. Her heart pumped faster and she knew that this was the kind of break she'd been working toward for a long time.

She checked her excitement as she realized the new assignment would take her away from a very personal investigation she'd been working on—the death of one of her closet childhood friends, Rainy Miller Carrington. Rainy had been Tory's orientation group leader when she'd first gone to Athena Academy as a nervous seventh-grader.

Tory had been invited to attend the mysterious Athena Academy for the Advancement of Women at the age of eleven. The unique seventh-through-twelfth-grade boarding school was set up similarly to famed military schools, but had no affiliation with the military.

Rainy, a senior, had been put in charge of Tory and five other girls other who, after a rough start, had come together to become lifelong friends despite being from very different backgrounds.

They'd named their group the Cassandras for the prophetess who was doomed never to be believed. Tory liked the irony of being a reporter and a Cassandra. In fact many of her Athena friends had gone into careers that involved uncovering the truth. The other Cassandras were FBI forensic scientist Alexandra Forsythe, private investigator Darcy Allen Steele, CIA Agent Samantha St. John, Air Force Captain Josie Lockworth and Kayla Ryan, a police lieutenant.

They'd bonded while they worked hard at Athena. Tory had enjoyed the female camaraderie and the competition. At home Tory had always had to outsmart her older brother, Derrick, who liked to play tricks on her. For the most part she and Derrick had a good relationship, but he'd definitely kept her on her toes when she'd been younger.

She had gone into network news because she'd realized early on that getting answers and putting together the pieces of a puzzle were things she was good at. Her classes in archery, marksmanship and martial arts had been invigorating, but she'd really excelled in the subjects that focused on criminal procedure and investigation. She'd briefly debated going into law but in the end had decided to become a journalist. She liked writing and photography and she had a talent for getting people to open up and talk.

She opened her e-mail and found one waiting from Josie, summarizing the findings of the Cassandras' investigation into Rainy's death. Tory and Josie were very close friends. They seldom had time to get together in person, but they communicated via e-mail often.

The e-mail was written with a military efficiency.

To: Cassandras
RE: Rainy Miller Carrington
Facts (Recap):

- In August, Rainy enacts the Cassandra promise, summoning all available Cassandras to Athens, AZ. Meeting set for the third Saturday in August at Principal Christine Evans's bungalow at Athena Academy, 2000 hours sharp. Kayla Ryan, Darcy Steele, Alex Forsythe and Josie Lockworth are present.
- Rainy dies in a car accident on her way to the meeting. Seat-belt failure contributed to the fatality. No evidence of tampering present.
- Alex attends Rainy's autopsy. She discovers that the appendectomy Rainy supposedly had in her first year at Athena never happened. Old ovarian scars show evidence of egg mining. Alex brings FBI agent Justin Cohen in on the investigation. Cohen's sister died twenty years ago in childbirth after becoming a surrogate mother, about nine months after Rainy's supposed appendectomy. Records show the baby died, as well. Cohen suspects Athena Academy of a conspiracy resulting in sister's death. No proof found.
- Kayla begins search of old medical records at Athena Academy for more information. Athena Academy continues to be under informal investigation. Nurse Betsy Stone potential suspect.

Stone was a nurse the academy at the time of Rainy's operation.

- Darcy finds ads for surrogate mothers in Arizona papers from the months before Rainy's operation. Hypothesis is that Rainy's eggs were used to make a child/children. Darcy finds Cleo Patra, a woman who answered the surrogate ad and subsequently gave birth to a baby girl. The child was kidnapped. Whereabouts unknown. Attempts made on Cleo's and Darcy's lives. Cleo now in hiding.

- Tory to investigate fertility clinic records for the time period surrounding Rainy's operation for any possible links.

- Messages left for Samantha St. John to apprise her of the situation. Sam in touch infrequently by e-mail. Whereabouts currently unknown.

Everyone please keep in touch with any new information.

Josie

Tory rubbed the back of her neck. Just before Rainy had graduated, all the Cassandras had made a vow that they would all come, no questions asked, if one of the Cassandras called for help. They'd called it the Cassandra promise. Rainy had been the first to call on it, and all of the Cassandras knew that the situation must have been dire indeed for Rainy to make that call.

Tory had been in Britain in July covering a major

development with Ireland when Rainy had placed the call to the Cassandras. Tory hadn't gotten the message until it was too late. Before she had a chance to respond, Kayla had called with the news of Rainy's death. Tory had returned to the States just in time to attend Rainy's funeral.

Tory was still coming to terms with Rainy's death. If only she'd known…

She sighed and rubbed the bridge of her nose. She couldn't go back in time and change things.

All the Cassandras were certain that Rainy's car accident could not have been accidental. Much to their horror, the facts they'd put together indicated that Rainy's death had something to do with Athena Academy.

Something that ex-Athena student and reporter for rival network ABS Shannon Conner had picked up on. Shannon had always been sneaky and a little underhanded when Tory and she had been at Athena.

In fact, Shannon had tried to frame Josie for theft, an event that had led Tory to the career she had today. The incident had become Tory's first investigative case. She'd used the skills she'd acquired at Athena in criminal profiling and investigating to solve the crime, finding evidence to prove that Shannon had been the perpetrator.

Shannon had become the only student ever to be expelled from the school. And Tory knew Shannon hadn't forgotten. She was always dogging Tory's heels. It was funny that they'd both chosen media as a career, but on one hand it made sense. That incident with Josie had changed both women and had forced them to look hard at what they wanted.

For Tory, it was to always be a voice for those without one. To uncover the stories that had to be told.

She wasn't sure what Shannon had taken away from the incident. But a few months ago, Shannon and her network had descended upon Rainy's funeral and had aired an interview in which Shannon had raised questions about Rainy being used for scientific experiments while in school at Athena.

Shannon's newscast had put the school in a bad light and had brought the school the unwanted publicity Athena had avoided since its founding more than twenty years ago. Tory had stepped in with a very upbeat piece about the school, which she hoped would counteract the negative publicity. But Shannon was still making noises about a follow-up on Athena, and Tory wasn't going to let Shannon get away with ruining the school. Loyalty was one of the cornerstones of Tory's life.

But even more important than neutralizing Shannon was finding out what had happened to Rainy, both now and in the past.

Darcy Steele had tracked down a surrogate mother who had carried a baby that might have been Rainy's. All the Cassandras were committed to finding the child. Tory had promised to look into the ads and use her news sources to look for leads through fertility clinic records.

Kids scared her on so many levels. Another plus to dating Perry was that he had two grown kids from a previous relationship and he wasn't looking to make her into a wife and mother. Tory freely admitted that settling down wasn't in the cards for her. There were too many stories for her to cover to willingly give up her career for a husband and kids.

But she would do everything in her power to find Rainy's baby. Tory frowned. That "baby" would be about twenty-one years old now. If he or she existed at all.

She'd researched a two-year window around the time the ads had run. And kept narrowing the search until she'd found something interesting—a break-in at a fertility clinic in Arizona about three months before Rainy's surgery. She wasn't sure it meant anything, so she'd sent the information to an old college friend, Lee Chou. Lee worked for the FBI crime lab in D.C. and was an expert at unraveling mysteries. Though Alex also worked for the FBI, she didn't know Lee. And Tory knew that because Alex's specialty was forensic science, Lee was going to be the man to get the information for her.

Tory dialed his number from memory.

"Chou," he said, answering his phone on the third ring. He sounded the same as he always did. Tired, brusque and maybe a little mean.

Not the kind of guy you wanted to piss off. And that might be why they'd become fast friends at Columbia. Tory had the kind of sunny personality that balanced out the more abrupt people of the world.

"Hey, it's Patton."

"Twice in the same week. To what do I owe the pleasure?" he asked. It had been at least six months since she'd seen him.

"I can't call to say hello?"

"You can, but you never do."

"Sorry. I've been busy."

"I know. Making quite a name for yourself. I saw that piece you did on Maurice Steele. Nice job. I was impressed."

"Thanks, Lee. I was glad it turned out well."

Maurice Steele was a Hollywood producer—and Darcy's soon-to-be ex-husband. He'd been possessive and abusive to Darcy, but Darcy and her son were now free of Maurice and the world knew the truth about the kind of man he was. He'd soon be on trial for murdering one of his financial backers, a crime Darcy had exposed while fighting to be free of Maurice once and for all.

Tory had intended to put together a follow-up piece that delved into the Hollywood myth that celebrities were above the law, but her story had been eaten by the editor's computer. The next evening Shannon Conner had gone on air with a similar story.

"Have you got anything for me yet?" Tory asked.

She heard the creak of his chair. She knew him well enough to guess that he'd probably propped his feet on his desk. "I'm not sure. I'm trying to track down a child that may not exist. This feels like one of those bizarre *X-Files* type cases that traces back to little green men."

She glanced at the picture of her and the Cassandras that had been taken on graduation day. It hung on her wall where she could easily see it.

"Chou, you've been watching too much TV. I have some old print ads that I received from a friend that might be connected to the burglary at the fertility clinic. Can I e-mail them to you?" she asked.

She addressed an e-mail to him, then scanned the old print ads that had led Darcy to the surrogate and attached them to the e-mail. She explained a little more of the background and what she knew about the situation.

"I'll look into it and get back to you."

"Thanks, Lee. I'm going to be out of the country for a few days, so contact me via e-mail if you find anything."

While she was on the Internet she sent a brief message to AA.gov. The Athena Academy alumni Web site had been created by several Athena grads. Along with maintaining the Athena student network, they worked with the intelligence community to provide couriers. Tory did some work for them because her job provided really good cover. She had a legit reason to be in many of the world's hot spots.

She let them know she was going to Puerto Isla, mentioned her flight number and then shut down her computer. She had to go home and pack.

Tory leaned back in her chair, crossed her booted feet and smiled to herself. This SEAL story was going to be the one to take her into the big leagues. She could feel it in her bones.

Chapter 2

"Tory Patton, please pick up the white courtesy phone. Tory Patton to the white courtesy phone."

Tory slipped her shoes back on and then gathered her laptop case and large carry-on. Having just passed through airport security, she had about forty minutes to waste before her flight took off. She found the white courtesy phone and gave her name.

"Your mother left a message for you. You can get hepatitis from the water, so watch what you drink. And that tunnel trick is getting old. Be careful."

"Thanks," Tory said. "Any other messages?"

"Just that one," the operator said with a chuckle.

Tory smiled. Her mother had called while Tory was on her way to the airport and had proceeded to give her usual safety lecture. Tory had pretended cell phone interference in the tunnel and had hung up on her. No matter how old she got, Evelyn Patton insisted on seeing Tory as about twelve. She made a mental note to call her mother from Miami. She hung up the courtesy phone, then turned and bumped into a man. He steadied her and leaned close.

"Tory Patton?"

"Who wants to know?" The guy was a little taller than she was in her two-inch heels. He had brown hair and wore a navy-blue trench coat. He subtly scanned the thin airport crowd as he held her arm.

"AA.gov."

She edged back from the guy, surprised that he'd contacted her out in the open like this. Usually courier drops were arranged via e-mail and done without any direct contact. But she knew there hadn't been time to set up a drop the usual way, and she assumed that this case was time sensitive.

"Can I see some ID?"

He sighed and pulled his wallet from his pocket showing her the American-eagle insignia that AA.gov used. She had the same leather card with the same insignia on it.

"Can't be too careful these days," she said. Rainy had always said not to trust appearances. *What am I missing here, Rainy?*

Tory found her old friend on her mind all the time lately. She knew it was because she still felt guilty for not being there when Rainy had called. She'd started talking to Rainy in her thoughts, as if her old mentor would somehow hear her and answer.

"There's an envelope for you inside this newspaper. Shred the instructions before getting on the plane. You're on a work visa, right?"

She nodded.

"Any problems, you know who to contact." He handed her the paper and left.

Tory stood there for a minute wondering why she continued to do these jobs. She didn't need the money the way she had when she'd been in college. But she knew in her heart that she did them because they validated all the hard work she'd done at Athena.

She tucked the paper under her arm and went to the Admiral's Club. Her frequent-flyer status assured her entrance. She went to the bar and got a gin and tonic before finding a seat in the corner away from the sparse crowd. It was a Wednesday, so there weren't too many people flying.

She opened the paper and Alexandra Forsythe's brother, Bennington, smiled up at her with a woman on each arm. Tory knew that Alex was more than a little frustrated that her older brother was so…shallow. A frustration that Tory couldn't relate to because her own brother, Derrick, was a DEA agent on the fast track to the top.

Alex was driven and didn't understand how someone who was related by blood didn't share that same drive. Ben said he'd been born to wealth and intended to take every advantage and opportunity that afforded him, which drove Alex crazy. But despite Ben's playboy lifestyle, he and Alex were very close.

Was it possible that Bennington was a changeling? Wearing a white dinner jacket and a smile that half the men in Hollywood would kill for, he looked utterly charming. But Tory knew better. She'd met Alex's brother several times, and the man had been totally annoying. He had been in the military for a short time but had said the tailoring didn't suit him.

His hair was swept back from his forehead, and he had a look in his blue eyes that promised decadence and pleasure. The caption of the photo said it had been taken in Manhattan at a charity event sponsored by his family's foundation.

Bennington had charisma, something that Tory had always thought was wasted on him. That kind of power should have gone to a man who would use it for more than his own ends.

She shook her head. Flipping the page, she saw the envelope. Tory glanced around to make sure no one was watching her. The tables nearby were empty. She opened the envelope. It contained a small leather pouch and a note addressed to her. Tomorrow night, Thursday, she was to meet her contact in Cabo de la Vela, a small mountain town on Puerto Isla.

The information included longitude and latitude numbers, as well as instructions for what she was supposed to wear. She was to give the contact the leather pouch and leave. She committed the information to memory.

One of the reasons Tory had come to the attention of the Athena Academy had been her photographic memory. She'd grown up in Placid Springs, Florida, a small ranching community, and the local weekly paper had done a story on Tory when she was ten, talking about how she could memorize anything and repeat it verbatim.

Entertainment had been hard to come by in those days, and Tory had been a main source for the town, which doted on the Pattons' only daughter. Her classes at Athena had honed her photographic memory and taught her to use it for intelligence gathering. She used it in her job at the network all the time.

She folded the newspaper and slid it and the leather pouch into her large carry-on bag. Then she walked to the office area in the lounge and shredded her directions. She walked out of the lounge without a backward glance, feeling the familiar excitement pumping through her veins.

Tory met up with her cameraman, Jay, in Miami. Their flight had been delayed overnight so it was Thursday morning when they arrived in Puerto Isla's capital, Paraiso, via an Air Mexico flight. Tory had been surprised at how crowded the flight was. Puerto Isla still had a State Department warning against travel because the new government, though more stable than the last, had yet to prove itself.

The coup four months earlier had brought an end to the reign of Diego Santiago. Alejandro Del Torro had taken power and established an interim military government. Tory had taken the time to do some Internet research on Del Torro last night in her hotel room. She'd also notified AA.gov that she'd be unable to make her courier drop until the following day.

Del Torro's government was getting different parties in place and would be holding elections within the next six months. The U.S. had sent troops to help restore order, but the majority of them had been pulled out in the past month. Tory knew from a conversation with her brother that the DEA still had agents in Central America and Puerto Isla.

The U.S. Embassy had backed the new leader because he favored the policy of eradicating the coca-leaf plant. Tory had spoken to Juan Perez, Puerto Isla's minister of foreign affairs, on the phone during her layover in Miami.

Minister Perez had said that many locals weren't happy with the new government's policy on the coca plant, though they did like the money that the U.S. was pouring into the economy. He invited her to tour his office while she was on the island. Tory planned to do just that. An interview with Perez would be a nice detail to the feature story on the navy SEAL. He'd agreed to speak to her this afternoon at the presidential palace in Paraiso.

Perez was also her main contact to connect with Thomas King. King had been found only a few days earlier and was in a military hospital in Paraiso, recovering from his harsh captivity. Tory was eager to get to the hospital and see King. Mr. Perez had warned her that King was still in pretty bad shape.

Perez hadn't answered any of her questions over the phone about how King had been found or why he'd still been imprisoned in the first place. But Tory didn't plan to let Perez dodge her questions when they met in person.

The hot island air brushed over her skin like a lover's hands. She shed her jean jacket and smiled at Jay.

"Not bad for November." The weather was so different from the chill of November in Manhattan. She closed her eyes, inhaling the fragrances of wildflowers and sea breeze. The freshness of the air reminded her of her parents' ranch and for a minute she felt as if she were back in Placid Springs and life was simpler.

"Not bad at all. I knew there was a reason you were my favorite reporter," Jay said.

"Because I brought you to a warm place in November?"

He just smiled at her. Jay moved with an easy grace through the airport terminal. He was almost six feet tall and had broad shoulders that tapered to a lean waist. Tory knew him to be a hard worker and a wicked poker player. He'd also spent the first few years of his career working at the Central American desk for the network. He was familiar with the people and the customs of this island nation.

"You say that to everyone." Tory liked Jay because he was easy to get along with and he was more of a photojournalist than just a cameraman. He'd gotten some film that was pure genius over the years. He was also incorrigible. He'd let Tory know a few times that he'd like to start something with her. But Tory had no interest in ruining a perfect reporter-cameraman relationship.

"Yeah, but with you I mean it."

"Ha." She deftly changed the subject. "Our visas should clear us through without too much problem."

They made their way through the airport. It wasn't as crowded as LaGuardia had been or even as bad as Miami International, where they'd connected, but there were people here. The line at customs was short, and Tory scanned the people waiting ahead of them. Suddenly she did a double take.

A familiar-looking blonde stood two people ahead of Tory. She had a few designer bags and the same Midwest generic American newscaster's accent that Tory did. *Shannon Conner.* How had she gotten there without Tory seeing her? She must have been on their flight.

Tory's reporter's mind started sorting through information and trying to find answers. Shannon must have flown first-class and gotten on at the last minute, so Tory and Jay hadn't spotted her. Was she following

Tory in the hopes of getting to a story before her? Or did she know where Tory was going? And if so, where was she getting her information?

Shannon showing up at the same location couldn't be a coincidence. This was the fourth time in as many weeks.

Tory suspected Shannon was still sore about getting kicked out of Athena. That had been a long time ago, and Tory had tried to put the incident behind her. However, Shannon had never really wanted to bury the ax. Except maybe in Tory's back.

In college, they'd both interned with the same television station, and it was there that Tory realized that Shannon still had it in for her. Not that Tory really cared. Their business was highly competitive, and having Shannon nipping at her heels or a half pace ahead of her really kept Tory focused on her career. She didn't plan on letting Shannon win.

"There's your buddy," Jay said. It was common knowledge in the industry that she and Shannon didn't get along.

"Very funny. Save my place?"

"Sure."

Tory got out of line and walked up to Shannon. Shannon was from Atlanta and always made Tory feel like a country bumpkin by comparison. Tory knew she wasn't. She carefully picked her clothes out at exclusive New York department stores so that she looked successful. But every time they met, she remembered her jeans and worn cowboy boots and how Shannon had made fun of her.

"Shannon?" Tory called.

Shannon pivoted to face her with a smug grin. She pushed her sunglasses onto her head and looked Tory over from head to toe. Tory felt rumpled and dirty from flying. Shannon looked as if she'd just stepped off a luxury jet.

"Tory, what are you doing here?" she asked.

"Working on a story. Puerto Isla is hot right now with the new regime in place and making new announcements every day."

"That's right, it is."

"Is that what you're doing here?" Tory asked.

"Of course."

Tory knew they were both lying and she sensed that Shannon was after the same story she was. If it had been any other reporter, Tory would have been tempted to fish around a little more for some information. But it wasn't.

"You don't usually handle world politics," Tory said at last.

"I'm trying to broaden my scope. My Athena story really made the network take notice of me."

"I'll bet. Going to do a story that focuses on the facts instead of sensationalizing them like you did with Athena Academy?"

"You're just jealous because the story got so much attention."

"I'm not jealous, Shannon. I'm angry because you showed up at my friend's funeral and tried to make the school sound like a top-secret breeding ground for freaks."

"Well, you managed to cover up the truth nicely."

"I managed to tell the truth. See if you can't remember what that is. Have you read the *Broadcast News Style* book lately?"

"I'm not a rookie. I know enough to get the job done."

"I hope so."

"You know, Patton, I never really cared for your attitude and I can't wait to take you down a peg or two."

"You're welcome to try."

"I intend to."

Jealous cow, Tory thought as she turned away and walked back to Jay. She should have said, *"I'm not going to try. I'm going to do it."*

"Happy reunion?"

"Why did I request you again?" she said, but she was smiling.

"You can't resist a man with a tattoo." He gestured to the intricate hawk on his arm.

"Yeah, that's it."

"Don't sweat Conner's appearance here. She's not half the reporter you are and she knows it."

"Thanks, Jay."

Jay moved to the customs agent to the left, and Tory was directed to the right. She handed her passport to the agent, who stamped it and checked her bag and said, *"Recepcion, Puerto Isla, Señorita Patton."*

Welcome, she thought. It was funny how countries always said that when you entered them whether they wanted you there or not. *"Gracias, señor."*

Jay and Tory rented a Jeep and made their way through the island traffic to the tourist district of Paraiso. The city had the old-world appeal of Cuba before Castro. Tory wished she had her still camera in her hand so she could capture the beauty of the island. But she wasn't here to photograph; she was here to investigate.

It was just after lunchtime when they arrived at the hotel. The hotel was in the Hilton chain and was in better shape than Tory had expected.

Shannon was at the front desk checking in when Tory and Jay walked through the lobby doors. Tory and Jay waited for her to finish her business and leave the lobby before they checked in. Tory left Jay in the lobby bar, where he said he'd be getting the lay of the land. But she had the feeling he just planned to get laid. He had taken a seat at a table with two beautiful, dark-haired women.

Tory planned to do some work. She didn't need Jay until tomorrow morning when she went to the hospital for the interview with Thomas King, since Perez had agreed to speak to her only off camera. She checked her watch. She still had three hours until she was supposed to meet with Perez.

Her room was on the second floor. She found it and

hung up her clothes, then settled at the small desk with her laptop. According to the desk clerk nothing happened in Puerto Isla until after the siesta time was over at 2:00 p.m. That gave Tory a little more than an hour to do some recon.

Shannon Conner wasn't getting this story. It went beyond anything resembling competition, straight to the heart of who Tory was. Something strange was going on in her life, and she was tired of Shannon showing up everywhere.

Tory started making notes and composed a list of questions to ask the islanders about the tension in Puerto Isla six months ago when the hostages had been taken and the navy SEALs sent in to rescue them.

What was the emotional climate? How did they feel about having the U.S. send its troops in? Did they back Del Torro's government? Were the hostages familiar to them?

Already the story was starting to form in her head, and she jotted down a few opening sentences. She could hear her own voice-over, introducing American viewers to the island paradise that had turned into Hell on Earth for Thomas King. She wrote a note to Jay about some cutaway shots she wanted him to get for the feature. She wanted to show the lush tropical forest and long, white sandy beaches they'd passed on their way here.

She worked for thirty minutes, doing some research on the Internet. But since she was here she wanted to

get out there with the Puerto Isla people and listen to
them talk. To try to understand what had happened
when Thomas King and his platoon had come to the
island.

She picked up the phone and called Jay's room. He
answered on the second ring.

"Matthews."

"Hey, no luck with the ladies?"

"I'm saving myself for you."

She chuckled. "Sure, you are. Listen, I want to go
interview some Paraiso citizens to get their views on
what's been going on here."

"Great. I'll meet you in the lobby in fifteen minutes.
How long are we going to be?"

"I'm not sure. I have a four-o'clock appointment
with Perez but he'll only speak to me off camera."

"I'll go with you anyway and do some pick-up shots
of the palace and surrounding area."

"I've made a list of shots I want you to get."

She changed into a pair of black trousers and a
short-sleeved black T-shirt. She pulled out a map of
Puerto Isla that she'd downloaded from the Internet.
They were staying in the former resort town of Paraiso,
now the island's capital. There were main roads from
the small airport and the large port into the city. The
island's coast was dotted with smaller towns and farms.
The middle of the island seemed uninhabitable.

Tory went out on the balcony. To the west, she could
see the high-rise condos that blocked the view of the

beach. To the east rose a large mountain. Leaning over the balcony railing, she studied the city as it started to wake up from siesta. People appeared on the sidewalks, and small European cars filled the cobblestoned streets.

She took her notebook and grabbed her jacket. Jay wasn't in the lobby when she arrived, so Tory approached the front desk, hoping to get some information from the young man about the hostage situation and the recent coup.

The desk clerk looked up in disinterest as she approached. Before she could ask him a question, the elevator doors opened and Shannon walked into the lobby.

She was dressed similarly to Tory but had her arm through a local man's. She gave Tory a superior look as she walked by. Tory ignored her.

Tory smiled at the desk clerk. He didn't smile back. She asked for directions to a local tavern and the docks. She hesitated, then asked, "Where is the prison?"

She took the map out of her bag. She knew that Thomas King had been held in one. "Could you mark it on the map for me?"

Finally he looked up at her and she read the fear in his eyes. He pushed the map back toward her. "You don't want to go there."

"Why not?" she asked.

"Not a nice place for a gringa."

"What about a gringo?" Jay asked, walking up beside Tory.

He leaned in, close to Tory. She hesitated for a moment and then shifted away from him. Jay always crowded her.

"Do you know where it is or not?" she asked.

The desk clerk searched her eyes for a minute and she didn't know what he was hoping to find. Finally he sighed and pulled out a street map of the city. His finger fell on a road near the edge of town that looked as if it ran into the jungle.

"Take Camino al Infierno. It dead ends at the guard shack."

She translated the road's name in her head. "Road to Hell." Well, it took more than a name to scare her.

Tory drove the Jeep through the streets of Paraiso. They stopped at an open-air market, and she surveyed the people who went about their business with little rushing around. The mood was laid-back and the steel-drum band that was set up on the corner playing added to it.

"What's the plan?"

"Do you have the Steadicam?" she asked. The Steadicam was a camera that didn't need a tripod but could be balanced and steadied on the cameraman's shoulder. Jay handled the camera with an ease that belied its heavy weight.

"Of course."

"You're fluent in Spanish, right?" Tory asked.

"Yes. I grew up in Little Havana, so I'm more fluent in the Cuban dialect, but I can get by. What do you want me to do?"

"Talk to that steel-drum band and see if they'll agree to be filmed. I think that will give our viewers a nice sense of the flavor of Paraiso. Oh, and I want to go back and film that slum we passed on the way from the airport, too."

"Will do. Where should I meet you?"

Tory glanced around the open-air market. It was comprised of rough wooden stalls and thatched roofs. There was a weather fountain that was dry but had a nice flowering stone in the middle of it. "Right there."

"Fifteen?"

She nodded, and they went their separate ways. Tory walked with the crowds for a minute, letting the language swell around her. Gradually her thought patterns began to change and she became accustomed to Spanish again. She listened to the conversation of two women about her age and realized that overprotective mothers were universal. These women were the equivalent of suburban mothers in America, with similar concerns about issues like schools, health insurance and child care.

Tory joined the conversation and sympathized with the two women. They chatted for a few minutes about families before Tory brought up the coup and the new government. The women were very vocal about their feelings that Del Torro wasn't any better than the man before him had been.

"Why not?" Tory asked.

"He's the puppet of the American government. Our people need a leader who can stand by himself."

Interesting. She knew that Del Torro was well liked by the U.S. because he enforced their policies, which weren't always popular in Central and South America. "I'm a reporter from UBC and we're doing a story on Puerto Isla. Would you be willing to let me interview you on camera?"

The women looked at each other and then at her. Abruptly the warm rapport she'd developed with them disappeared. "No."

"How about off camera?" she asked. But the women only shook their heads and walked away. It was the same with everyone she spoke to. They were living in a military state, and though Del Torro was better than Santiago had been, no one was willing to take a chance of speaking out against him.

When she got back to the fountain, she found Jay lounging in the sun. "No luck?"

"They all had plenty to say, but off camera. Can you just film the market and the people coming and going? I'll summarize what I learned and do a voice-over."

Jay nodded and then went to get his shots. Tory thought she saw Shannon in the crowd of shoppers, but when she moved closer to look, she couldn't find her rival. When Jay returned they headed over to the presidential palace for Tory's meeting with Perez.

The palace was a large stone structure that overlooked the port. It was a fortress that had been built to withstand attacks from the sea by pirates. There were cannons on the walls, and Tory felt for a minute that she was back at St. Augustine on her fourth-grade Florida-history field trip.

Jay parked the Jeep on the street and got out when she did.

"What are you doing?"

"Coming with you."

"Stay here."

He shrugged his shoulders and returned to the Jeep. Perez had been friendly to a certain point, but he'd been very clear that he didn't want to speak to anyone but Tory. And she needed him. Needed to find out exactly what was going on with King.

"I shouldn't be long."

She entered the building and gave her name to the receptionist, who invited her to sit down. Tory took a seat on one of the hardwood chairs and went over her questions for Perez.

The most important one being why had it taken the government so long to locate King? She also wanted Perez to arrange a visit for her and Jay to the prison, and perhaps an interview with the warden.

A door opened down the hall and Tory glanced up. A man was walking toward her. He looked familiar, and she ran through faces in her head, trying to place him. He was tall, probably about six feet and had blond hair with a bit of silver at his temples. He looked like

Robert Redford. The distance was too far for her to see his eye color, but he carried himself with confidence and an easy style that spoke of success.

He glanced up at her, smiling at first. Tory smiled back and stood up. He froze when he noticed the notepad in her hands and then turned to the left out of her view.

Tory sat back down, jotted the physical description of the man on her notepad and put a question mark next to his name.

"Who was that?" she asked the receptionist.

Before the woman could answer, Juan Perez arrived. He was a few inches taller than her. He had dark hair and olive-toned skin. He wore battle fatigues and combat boots.

"Señorita Patton?"

"Sí."

"I'm Juan Perez. Welcome to Paraiso. I'm sorry to have kept you waiting."

"No problem."

"Let's go into my office where we can talk."

Tory followed him down the marble hallway into an office that overlooked the ocean. The office was sparsely furnished with a battered-looking desk. Perez gestured to one of the guest chairs. Tory sat down on the edge and had her pen poised ready to start asking questions.

The phone rang before she could.

"Perez," the minister said into the phone.

He listened for a few minutes, glanced at Tory and then hung up the phone.

"I'm sorry, Miss Patton. But something has come up and I won't be able to speak to you today."

"We'll set up another time, then. Tomorrow?"

"I'm afraid this business will keep me tied up for…some time."

"Okay. Then tell me where King is being held so that I can set up a time to interview him."

"I'm sorry, but that will no longer be possible."

"What are you talking about? You called my network."

"I'm afraid that was a mistake."

Perez quickly showed her the door. No matter what questions she asked, he remained stubbornly reticent. A few minutes later she was standing alone under the hot late-afternoon sun of Puerto Isla, wondering what the hell was going on and why the invitation to an exclusive interview had suddenly been revoked.

Chapter 3

The next morning Tory woke up ready to work. After her disastrous meeting with Perez, she and Jay had gone to the prison to see where King had been held. The guard at the prison hadn't been any more cooperative than Perez had been. Jay had gotten a few long shots that they'd use when they edited the piece. Tory was beginning to feel that her exclusive interview with King wasn't going to come through.

Shannon had been in the lobby when Tory and Jay had returned, but Tory had ignored her and returned to her room to contact Cathy Jackson in UBC's research department. She'd spent thirty minutes on the phone describing the man she'd seen in the palace hallway and asking Cathy to pull information on Perez, Del Torro and Puerto Isla.

Tory had finally realized that the man she'd seen in the presidential palace was Chris Pearson. Pearson was a good friend of James Whitlow, the president of the United States. And many observers of the White House had noted Pearson's influence on the U.S. president. Tory tucked that away for later.

This morning the sun shone brightly through the gap in the room's blackout drapes. Tory stretched her arms over her head, remembering the story she'd read in the newspaper about the hostage incident earlier that year. It had been a small article in the world-news section saying only that four hostages had been killed on Puerto Isla by a group of local guerrillas.

According to the information she'd retrieved from her e-mail last night, Thomas King's SEAL team had been dispatched to rescue those hostages. What had gone wrong?

She knew they'd been based out of Little Creek, Virginia. During her three-hour layover in Miami she'd placed a call to the base there and spoken to Lieutenant Joe Peterson in the public-affairs office. He'd given her strictly the facts, which she'd passed on to Cathy in research for follow-up. All he'd really said was that the navy was very happy to find King alive. But she hadn't been satisfied with the answers she'd received.

They were, of course, thrilled that Thomas King was alive and recovering in a hospital in Paraiso. The extent of his injuries had been unknown to Peterson, but he did indicate that King had been starved and beaten.

She had a profile of the team that had been sent in. As she looked at the military ID photos that accompanied each name and short bio, her heart ached that only one of them had survived.

She'd pressed Peterson, trying to find out why King hadn't been moved to a U.S. airbase, and had been very politely told that King was a guest of the Puerto Isla government.

Someone didn't want him to leave, but who and why? Perez had definitely been in favor of her interview when she'd called him from Miami. What had changed when she arrived on the island?

She wondered if it was injury-related starvation, which could take a terrible toll on the body. The man had been in prison for six months. The only other reason Tory could think of was that he'd seen something he wasn't supposed to. But what?

When she'd spoken to him on the phone, Juan Perez had alluded to the fact that King wasn't well enough to move.

She felt a sense of urgency to get to Thomas King. She didn't question it. Trust your gut. It was something Rainy had said to her many times when she'd been trying to figure out a puzzle. And her gut was usually right.

Three policemen stood in the entrance to the coffee

shop just off the lobby talking to Jay. He caught her eye and tilted his head back sharply. Tory ducked behind a large potted plant and edged closer to Jay.

"...Señorita Patton," said the tallest of the guards. He was dirty and unshaved and a long, wicked-looking scar curved across his cheekbone, disappearing into his oily whiskers.

"*¿Cuáles el problema?*" Jay asked the guards.

"What's the problem?" he'd asked. And Tory leaned a little closer, trying to make out the guard's response.

"*...para el comportamiento sospechoso,*" the guard said.

Suspicious behavior? Great. She wondered if one of the people she'd spoken to yesterday in the market had called the cops on her. She hadn't even gotten started yet. Sinking back against the potted plant, she waited until she heard the guards leave. They'd probably stake out her room and wait for her to return.

Well, she'd known that her exclusive story had some risks. She thought briefly about packing up her stuff and heading back home. Tyson would understand. But Tory wondered if she'd ever be able to look herself in the eye again.

She wanted to visit—as a journalist, not as a guest— the prison where King had been held. The story was flowing through her veins. And though it might be dangerous to stay on Puerto Isla, she knew that nothing would satisfy her until she figured out the puzzle that was this exclusive interview with a SEAL.

She peered around the plant and saw that the lobby was clear. She hurried out the front door of the hotel, her pulse pounding and her hands shaking. She wasn't used to evading the local cops. A hand snaked out and grabbed her arm as she exited the hotel.

She jerked her arm free and spun around, hitting her assailant with a jab. She tried to lessen the pressure when she realized it was Jay.

He grunted and rubbed his jaw. His breath smelled like coffee and mints.

"You're a dangerous woman to know, Patton," he said under his breath. He pivoted so that she was pressed up against the side of the hotel wall and his body shielded hers from view. A little too close for friendly working-relationship comfort.

"Sorry about that," she said, stepping sideways and away from his body. Jay was her co-worker and she reminded herself that she was involved with Perry. She was feeling things she wouldn't normally feel if they'd been on her home turf.

He sighed and leaned against the wall next to her. He thrust his hands deep into the pockets of his pants.

"I've done worse damage tripping over a chair," he said with a wry shrug.

"So *la policía* are after me?"

He gave her a wry look beneath his eyelashes. "Yeah, who'd you tick off?"

The list was short and she had a feeling that this problem had followed her from New York. "It could have been one of the people I spoke to at the market-place. But I've got to be honest—I don't think they like the police."

"Yeah, but I got the feeling the locals don't like the *americanos* that much, either."

"You didn't sound American," she said, then had another thought. "I thought I saw Shannon following us yesterday." Did Shannon hate her enough to throw her to the island militia, which pretended to be all that stood between Puerto Isla and lawlessness? Tory knew the answer and she suspected Jay did, as well.

"Do you think Shannon called them?"

He shrugged. Reaching out, he tucked a strand of her hair behind her ear. "You do look very American."

She waggled her eyebrows at him. She'd been in scary situations before. She'd never forget the first night she'd spent in the maximum-security prison for her story on women behind bars. This wasn't any different. She'd done nothing the Puerto Isla cops could hold her on.

"I'm good at wiggling out of tight spots," she said.

"Let's hope you don't have to use that skill while you're here."

"I want to go to the hospital where King is being held and see if we can't get our interview tonight." She'd made another call to Perez and had flat out told him she wasn't leaving the island without her interview. In fact, he could have sent the police to arrest her. But he'd reluctantly told her to call again in the morning. He'd see what he could do.

What if Del Torro's government didn't want her to see King until he'd recovered from his time in their prison? She thought it would be in their favor to demonstrate how different they were from Santiago's government. But Perez had done an abrupt change in position in the past twenty-four hours. And Tory knew that she was working on a short clock. She needed to get to King, and quickly.

"You got it, boss lady. I'll grab my camera gear and meet you here."

They pulled up to the hospital where Thomas King was being treated just after lunchtime.

Jay parked the vehicle and they headed toward the building. Two men with AK-47 assault riffles stood at attention at the entrance, despite the fact that it was a public hospital, not a military one. Considering the fact that there was still a curfew and guerrilla unrest on the island, the guards weren't unexpected. But they did give her pause as she walked toward them.

There was something unnerving about men in uniform with guns. Tory put on her most charming smile and approached them. *"¡Hola! Soy Tory Patton con UBC. Estoy aquí ver a un paciente americano."*

"Ningunos visitantes permitieron adentro hoy."

No visitors, interesting. She'd hoped they'd just let her in. "I'm with the press and spoke yesterday to Juan Perez. Is there someone here I can speak to?"

"No."

"I'm just going to go inside and talk to the doctor in charge, okay?" Tory said. From past experience, she knew that, if you kept talking and walking, usually you could get in anywhere.

"No visitors." Both of the guards stepped closer together, blocking her path.

"Okay," she said, backing away.

"That was a little weird," Jay said once they were out of earshot of the guard.

"Yeah, why wouldn't they let us in?" she asked.

"The police captain who was asking for you mentioned that they are enforcing a strict curfew."

"What time? It's only the afternoon."

"I know. I don't think things are going as smoothly for the new government as we were led to believe."

"Me, either. If we have time, we'll try again to shoot some tape on the street talking to the citizens about the new government."

She and Jay got back in the Jeep. Tory glanced over and noticed the guards still watching them. "Damn, this ticks me off. I'm not going back to the States without this story."

"So what's next? Come back later?"

"Did you bring the hidden-camera unit I used for the prison story?" Tory asked. The hidden camera actually looked like a purse and had a switch that she could flip to record.

"Yes. I wasn't sure what the situation was going to be like here."

"Jay, I love you."

"Ha, you say that to all the guys."

"Yeah, but with you I mean it."

He climbed over the seat and dug around in his camera gear until he found the camera and small handbag that went with it. Tory shot some test film of Jay climbing back into the front seat. She rewound the film and played it back.

"This looks good. Okay, drop me off around back. I'm going to make sure King's really in there."

"I'll park up there and wait for you." Jay gestured to a park a block away, overlooking the ocean. "If you're not back in thirty minutes I'm coming in after you."

"I don't think it'll come to that."

Tory got out of the Jeep at the corner, and Jay drove up the block to park and wait.

The afternoon sun was weakened by storm clouds gathering over the mountains. Tory walked as if she had a purpose and a reason to enter the building. She approached the ER entrance of the hospital and saw two armed guards there, as well.

She ducked back in the shadow of the building before they could spot her. *Help me out here, Rainy.*

A minute later she saw a man with a nasty-looking wound in his chest walking toward the hospital. He was held upright by the swarthy woman under his arm. Two bedraggled kids followed behind her.

There were a couple of teenage girls in the family,

as well. The girls were taller than Tory was, and she was able to walk just a few steps behind them and blend into the family.

Thank you, Rainy.

Tory followed the family to the nurses' station and stood back while they were helped by the one nurse on duty. She led the family to a small partitioned area.

Tory glanced around quickly. Several people sat in chairs in the waiting area, and a doctor in scrubs walked past the desk and down another hallway.

Tory hurried behind the desk and shifted through the papers on the desk. She wasn't sure if King's name would be used on file or not. He'd been rescued only three days ago. She assumed he'd be in the critical-care unit.

She scanned the hospital layout and found that those units were on the fourth floor. She walked around the desk as a nurse reappeared.

"Can I help you?" the woman asked in Spanish.

"No, thanks." Tory got on the elevator and went to the fourth floor.

She stepped off the elevator and came face-to-face with two armed guards.

"Este piso es fuera de límites."

Tory smiled at the men and got back on the elevator. She went down one floor. She asked where the stairs were and climbed back up to the fourth floor.

She cautiously opened the door and saw the guards still at their post in front of the elevators. She wished she had a doctor's coat but she didn't know where they'd be stored here, if at all. Maybe she could find some surgical scrubs to wear.

She eased out into the hallway and kept close to the wall. She felt as if she had a huge orange neon sign on her back. Her heart beat so rapidly that she was convinced Jay could hear it a block away. Finally she turned the corner away from the guards.

She opened the door to the first room on the left and found it empty. She closed the door and started toward the next door.

"¡Parada!"

Tory glanced over her shoulder and saw one of the guards from the elevator. She sprinted away from him around another corner, dashing into the first open doorway and shutting the door. She scanned the dark room. It was empty. *I'm going to have a heart attack.*

A pair of arms came around her. A hard-gloved hand clamped over her mouth, and her head was tilted back at an uncomfortable angle. The body behind hers was hard, masculine and smelled too damned good.

Tory knew there was no rule that bad guys had to smell bad, but she thought there should be. Her instincts took over. She lifted her left leg and brought her heel down hard on her attacker's instep, but he didn't even groan at the impact. Instead he brought one of his legs around hers, trapping her. She tried to move but she was surrounded by his body.

She heard running in the hall. She tried to glance

over at her captor but couldn't until he released her jaw. Her eyes widened as she recognized the man holding her. His grip loosened as he identified her, as well.

"What the hell are you doing here?" Bennington Forsythe asked.

"I think that's a question I should be asking," Tory said. She scarcely recognized this Bennington. Instead of flawlessly cut designer clothing, he wore a black T-shirt and jeans. But the biggest change was his expression. Gone was the charming man-about-town and in his place was a dangerous man who made Tory wary.

Footsteps sounded right outside the door. Bennington cursed under his breath. Grabbing her wrist, he pulled her across the room and into a closet.

"Quiet," he said in a whisper that carried no farther than her ears.

Tory stood tensely next to her friend's brother, her mind spinning with a totally new puzzle. Bennington Forsythe—international playboy or spy?

Tory was still trying to process what had happened. One minute she was running from an armed guard; the next she was standing nose to nose with one of the best-known playboys in the Western Hemisphere. Had she taken a turn and stumbled into Alice's rabbit hole?

"Bennington, what are you doing here?"

"Not now."

One of the door guards entered the room, walking

past their hiding place in the closet. The door was partially open, and she could discern the shadows of the men as they searched the room.

Their shapes were large and bulky. Tory closed her eyes and slowed her breathing the way she did for yoga, focusing very carefully on making sure that her body relaxed from the sprint into the building.

Bennington kept his hand over her mouth. Now that the shock of seeing him was rubbing off, her training from her Athena days was kicking in. She heard the men moving in the room and knew the danger implicit in being caught. She'd been the one running from them.

Actually she'd probably have to rescue Bennington if they were discovered. Despite his long-ago military training, the hardest he'd exercised recently would probably have been in bed with those two supermodels he'd been photographed with. She reached behind her and felt along his belt to see if he was armed.

His thumb rubbed against her cheekbone, and for a minute Tory totally forgot everything else. They were alone in a small, dark space. Deprived of sight, she felt her other senses were on hyperalert.

Tingles spread down her body from his caressing thumb. This was the Ben she knew. A charming Casanova with a girl in every port. God, he was an idiot to be on Puerto Isla. But she guessed he wasn't here for the sport fishing, though it was some of the best in the world.

The arm he had around her waist tightened, and he

pulled her more fully back against him. He spread his fingers and she felt his touch at the bottom of her breast. She shifted in his arms. His hand moved up over her ribs, his touch hot through the layer of her thin cotton T-shirt.

She stepped down on his instep again. He didn't say a word but tightened his grip on her.

Even though two thugs were less than a few feet from them, her mind filled with sexy images of her and Bennington. She needed some space.

She bit his palm when he didn't move his hand, but he didn't drop it. She still had on her backpack so they weren't pressed too closely together, but he seemed to surround her. He was solid muscle. Maybe he'd had more recent training than she'd thought.

Using his grip on her, he tipped her head back and whispered straight in her ear. "Quiet."

The one word was a command. She nodded to let him know she'd understood. With all those muscles, even if he didn't have martial-arts training, he'd be able to take care of one of the guys. Quickly she turned, reaching for his waist to see if he was armed or wearing a holster.

Ben grabbed her hand.

"What are you doing?" he asked in that soundless whisper again, his hot breath grazing her ear with each word he spoke.

"Getting ready to rescue you," she whispered back. Once again she reached for his waist.

"Patton, don't push me," he hissed. He captured her hand in another one of his unbreakable grips.

"Oh, why not?"

A chair scraped across the floor in the room, and Tory froze. She strained away from Ben, ready to confront the men searching the room. But he pulled her deeper into the recess of the closet.

"Enough."

She felt him move around her and saw the glint off the barrel of his gun as he pushed her behind him. So he was armed.

The sliding door scraped along the track as one of the men pushed it open. He played the flashlight over the interior with clumsy skill. A voice called out from the hallway, and the guard turned just before the flashlight would have illuminated their spot. The guard muttered something in Spanish and retreated from the room.

Tory waited until they could no longer hear the guards, then pushed her way past Bennington, intent on getting some answers. She stepped out of the closet and turned on him. "What was that all about?"

"Keep your voice down—they could come back."

"I know that." Damn, he'd made her forget her Athena Academy training.

"What are you doing here?" he asked. Every line in his body was tense. He vigilantly watched the door. Tory couldn't reconcile the man standing before her with the man she knew as Alex's brother.

"I'm looking for Thomas King. I came here to interview him."

"How did you know he was here?" His eyes narrowed, she felt caught under his eaglelike glare.

"My boss got a call from the minister of foreign affairs, Juan Perez. I don't think it's been leaked to every network yet."

"It shouldn't have even been leaked to you."

"How do you know that? And what are you doing here, Bennington?"

Before he could answer, they heard footsteps approaching again. The person stopped outside their door, and Tory dropped into a fighting stance as the doorknob turned.

"Stay behind me, Ben. I have a third-degree black belt in tae kwon do. I'll protect you."

"Like hell. You Athena grads think you can take on the world one-handed," Ben said.

"We can."

"Not today. I've got a gun, and a gun trumps a black belt any day."

Chapter 4

Tory didn't like taking a back seat to Ben, but she hadn't made it to the top of a very competitive profession by making stupid choices. And though she wasn't sure of his abilities, he had a point—guns did trump martial arts.

He motioned for her to stand to the left of the door as he glanced around the room. She did as she was ordered.

He kept the barrel of his M-9 pointed toward the door. "You know how to use that thing?"

He didn't look at her as he took a pillow from the bed and held it in front of the gun barrel, then moved into position on the right side of the door. She realized he'd been searching for a silencer so as not to announce their presence to the guards searching the hospital for her.

"Believe it or not, men trained outside of Athena have some ability with weapons."

"Did I offend your manhood?" she asked. Ben knew a lot about Athena because his and Alex's grandfather Charles Forsythe was one of the academy's founders.

He did look at her this time, and even in the shadowed room she could make out his cocky grin. "Not yet."

He edged forward and she stayed in position, poised to attack. She remembered midnight training sessions at Athena in which she'd run through the dark, wooded area outside of teacher housing, knowing that other students, all black belts, were waiting to take her down. The exercise had honed her reflexes and stealth skills.

The door opened and a nurse froze in the doorway. Before she could speak, Tory reached past Ben and pulled the woman into the room with them.

"We won't hurt you."

Her eyes widened and she started to scream. Tory clamped her hand over the woman's mouth and pinched her carotid artery. The woman slumped against her. Tory took her under the armpits and laid her on the bed.

"Let's go," Ben said.

"I need to get to Thomas King. Something weird is going on with him. I can sense it."

"Why are you concerned about King?" Ben watched her with narrowed eyes.

She was surprised that he knew who King was.

Some pieces of the puzzle that was Ben Forsythe were morphing shape. "Why are you here in the same hospital as he is? And why are you armed? What do you know about him?"

"Nothing really," Ben said.

"Or if you do, you're not saying, right?"

"Tory, just pretend this never happened," he said, gesturing to the room and himself.

"You know that as a journalist I can't ignore this story, Ben. I'm not leaving the hospital until I'm sure King is here and he's unharmed."

"The less you know the safer you'll be."

"I've already started asking questions. And I'm not going to stop until I have this story figured out." Tory moved past Ben, intent on searching the floor and finding out where Thomas King was.

"I was afraid you'd say that. King's being moved tonight." Ben stopped her with a hand on her arm.

She was surprised he gave her the information. "Where to?"

"A more secure location."

"Ben, what are you doing here?"

"Listen, I'm kind of busy. Can we talk later, Patton?"

"Right."

Ben tucked his weapon into his ankle holster, and they left the room. The corridor outside wasn't busy, and Ben glanced both ways before leading her toward the stairwell.

"I don't want to—"

"Trust me, Patton. You'll still get your exclusive but you need to get out of here now before those guards come back."

She nodded. Ben was tall and ruggedly good-looking in this light. He scarcely resembled his newspaper pictures. A beard covered the bottom half of his face, he wasn't grinning and his eyes didn't have that vacant expression he usually wore. In fact, he seemed like a highly trained military man.

Funny that he'd never really looked muscular in his evening wear.

"I thought you left the military years ago," she said as they went down the stairs.

"Who says I didn't?"

"I'm trying to put the puzzle together, Forsythe. And most of the pieces don't fit."

"Then don't force them." He wrapped his arm around her waist and walked out of the hospital past the guards as if he owned the place.

Once they were away from the entrance, Tory tried to move away but Ben wouldn't let her. He pulled her against his body as they walked around the corner of the building.

He was pressed all along the side of her body. Her face was level with his chest and she leaned her head against him for a moment, guessing that he wanted them to look like a couple as they got away. He smelled good and clean, and for a second she wanted to rest there. To let her heart stop pounding like crazy.

Give her a lying politician or an apologetic Hollywood superstar who'd been busted for using cocaine and
she was okay. But running and hiding from *el policía*
who hated americanos made her feel vulnerable. Something she'd vowed a long time ago to never be.

As soon as they were out of sight of the guards, she
forced herself to shift away from Bennington. Hell, he
was Alex's useless brother. What the was going on here?

She stopped and turned to stare up at him. "What
are you doing on Puerto Isla?"

"What do you think I'm doing here?"

"It's a little too dangerous for you to come down
here to chase after your love bunnies, so I'm not sure."

He gave her a half smile that took her breath away.
"Nice opinion you have of me."

"I didn't know you cared."

"I don't."

A patrol of two guards rounded the corner. Ben
tensed and swore.

He backed her against the wall. His mouth moved
over hers with none of the skill and finesse she'd have
expected of him. Instead she was overwhelmed with
raw passion and a primal feeling that welled up deep
in her soul.

His free hand cupped her butt and pulled her fully
into the cradle of his thighs. One of his legs slipped between hers. He had her completely protected with his
body, and though the threat was imminent she still responded to the passion in him.

It had been a long time since a man had kissed her like Bennington was doing right now.

"*Helada. ¿Qué usted está haciendo?*" one of the guards called out.

Ben lifted his head, rubbed his lips over hers one time and then glanced over at the guard who'd asked them what they were doing.

"*El intentar conseguir una cierta acción,*" Ben said with a grin. Then lowered his head to hers again.

The guard laughed and walked away, wishing Ben luck. Ben continued to hold her until the men disappeared, and she did her best to ignore the racing through her bloodstream.

She was here on the job, dammit. And nothing—certainly not Bennington Forsythe—was going to mess with that.

The afternoon air was thick with the smell of hibiscus, something that always reminded Tory of her mother's house and the bushes that grew under her childhood bedroom window. She pulled back from Ben. He kept her loosely tucked to his side.

He put on a pair of sunglasses, shielding his eyes from her. She wasn't sure she could trust him. He hadn't said he was in the military, and the Ben she knew could very easily be down here on a lark. Working—or rather playing—at some dangerous game that involved little or no ethics.

"I can see why you have a reputation as a ladies'

man," she said lightly. She edged farther away from him. But his hand on her waist stopped her.

"There's a lot more smoke to my reputation than substance." She pushed his hand off. He put it back, more firmly. He scanned the area searching for something. Backup? More attackers? She didn't know.

"Actually, Forsythe, I'm beginning to think there's more substance than you'd like the world to see." That wasn't very subtle, but she was on an adrenaline jag from her near escape with armed police.

"There isn't, Patton." His voice was devoid of its earlier commanding tone. This was the Ben she'd run into a few times in Manhattan. Society's golden boy, who flitted from woman to woman and party to party with little care.

"Why are you doing this?" she asked. His hand still gripped her waist. She'd always been a little intrigued by Alex's brother.

"You heard what I told the guards," he said.

"Trying to get a little action? Ben, you're hopeless." She tilted her head back and tried to read his eyes, but it was impossible with those dark shades and his guarded expression.

"Nah, baby. I'm just an all-American male." He ran one finger down the side of her face. She knew he was playing her. Using the spark of attraction that had developed between them to distract her from the questions she was dying to ask.

"I won't stop asking until you tell me what you're doing here."

Ben stepped away from her. He took her hand, leading her away from the hospital.

"You're not still on about that, are you?" he asked. He pushed his hands through his thick hair and pivoted away from her.

"I never really left it," she said softly.

"Well, forget it, Tory, and forget me. Get yourself off this island as quick as you can. This isn't the place for you. Who let you come down here?"

He didn't sound like Society Sam now. He was pure pissed-off male and Tory bit the inside of her mouth to keep from smiling. She wondered if he'd ever be able to fool her with his charming rogue's smile again.

"Ben, it's the twenty-first century. No one let me come. My station sent me. I was promised an exclusive."

He nodded. "Go back to Miami. I'll make sure you talk to King there."

"How can you ensure that? Are you still with the military?"

"Never mind me. Just get back to your hotel, pack your stuff and get your sweet ass off this island."

"My sweet ass?" Tory wanted to smile at him but wasn't going to. Her mind was swirling with questions and half-formed answers. She needed to write this encounter down on paper. She thought better with a pen in her hand.

"It's a phrase."

"One most guys are smart enough to keep to themselves."

"I haven't heard any complaints."

She narrowed her eyes and stepped away from his touch. "I'm not leaving the island. This interview is my chance to reach the next level in my career. And it's not like I don't have the training to handle this type of situation."

"God save me from Athena women. Seriously, Tory, forget you saw me here."

"I don't think I'll be able to do that," she said. There was something different about Ben in her mind now, and she knew she'd never forget his rock-hard body or his skill and knowledge in getting them away from the hospital.

"Try real hard. You're a smart lady—you should be able to figure out something."

"That's right, Bennington, I am a smart lady and I've finally realized that something about you doesn't add up."

"Let me know when you figure out what it is," he said. "Where are you staying?"

"Near the airport."

"Where's your car?" he asked.

She gestured in the direction where Jay was still parked. She hoped.

"I'll see you safely to your car."

"I can handle walking to my car by myself," she said.

"Be careful. Even Athena graduates sometimes find themselves in over their heads."

"I know that."

"I wish you'd leave."

"I'm not going to until I talk to Thomas King. I've had some time to think about his situation, and nothing adds up."

"Like what?" he asked. She couldn't tell if he was curious or ticked off because she refused to let it go.

"Well, how did the guerrillas ambush an entire SEAL platoon? You know how well trained the SEALs are. One or two causalities I can believe, but the entire team?"

"They are highly trained. But even highly trained men can make a mistake."

"Is that what happened?"

"How would I know? I'm here for the sun, sand and beautiful babes."

"Thirty minutes ago I would've believed that."

"It's in your best interest to believe it again. When are you supposed to meet King?"

"Well, I kind've got officially uninvited to interview him, but Perez is meeting with me tomorrow morning."

"Be careful, Patton. Someone doesn't want King to talk to you," he said, and she couldn't tell if he was warning her or threatening her.

"You?"

"We wouldn't be having this conversation if that were the case."

"You don't scare me. I've got my Athena training, don't forget," she said with a wry grin.

"What does scare you?" he asked, his playboy smile fixed firmly in place.

She wasn't going to admit to fears to this man who'd implied that he might have killed her if that had been his order. She tossed her hair. "Nothing."

She walked away without looking back. And though she'd never admit it, she was glad Jay was in the Jeep.

The afternoon was balmy and she paused in the shade for a moment to tip her head back and just breathe. She wasn't as brave as her Athena pals. Her hands were still trembling. It's just an adrenaline let-down. But it felt like fear, and she didn't like being reminded that failure here could have higher consequences than just being busted back to the local television station.

Going the distance meant doing things you didn't want to do. She wasn't weak and she wouldn't give up. No one was going to deter her. Not even herself.

Thanks, Rainy, for making sure I paid attention at school. She smiled to herself and fancifully imagined Rainy by her side, covering her báck on Puerto Isla.

She must be more tired than she thought. In fact, she was bone weary. Her limbs felt heavy and her mind was buzzing with everything she'd learned today. Actually, with everything she hadn't been able to answer. Ben Forsythe was an enigma. How was he connected to King?

Thomas King was her priority. Why was he being moved? And why was the government suddenly refusing to let her see him? Something wasn't right. She wished she'd brought some kind of weapon with her. She felt ill equipped to handle the situation.

Thank God, Jay was waiting for her right where he'd promised. She climbed in and made a show of getting situated while she gathered her thoughts.

Jay shifted the vehicle into gear, and it bumped its way over the pothole-filled road. Tory stretched her arms over her head and tried to focus.

Thomas King had been in prison for six months. The new government leader, Alejandro Del Torro, the interim president, had rescued him. Del Torro had been outraged to realize that American POWs were being tortured in the prison. Which begged the question—why were they now refusing to grant her access to King? They had been the ones to call Tyson.

"Jay, I think I need to talk to President Del Torro instead of Perez. We'll go to the presidential palace in the morning."

"You're the boss."

"Doesn't it seem odd to you that everything is more complicated than it should be?" she asked. She needed to talk her ideas out to see if they had any substance. Usually she'd bounce ideas off of Perry or her boss, but Jay was the only one who was seeing what she saw.

"Yeah." Jay pulled a cigarette from his pocket and

lit it. He inhaled deeply and then turned toward her. The smoke circled his head.

"What's up?" Tory asked Jay when he pulled the Jeep to a stop a few miles away from the hospital.

"I had another visit from *el policía* captain while you were breaking and entering."

"Just entering—no breaking."

"I'm glad you think this is funny."

She didn't. "They came up to you in the car?"

"No, I'd stepped out to have a cigarette."

"Why was he looking for me?" she asked. It wasn't the first time she'd ruffled feathers, but it was the first time she'd done it before she'd really started asking questions.

"A woman called in an anonymous tip that you were here to broker a weapons deal with some drug runners."

Tory froze. "Shannon."

"He didn't say, but it makes sense. You haven't had time to cultivate any other female enemies—have you?"

"Not that I know of." Tory had the chills. Rivalry was one thing, but this was more than rivalry. Drug runners and arms dealers weren't very nice people, and if she'd gone to jail on those charges, she'd have been severely beaten and probably raped. The law on Puerto Isla was still too used to doing what it wanted. She'd heard tales from the people she'd talked to in the marketplace.

Did Shannon hate her so much?

Shannon had gone too far this time. The next time she saw Shannon, Tory was going to have it out with her. Scooping Tory's stories was one thing; sticking third-world cops on her trail was another matter entirely.

"I gave the police some money and moved the car. When I circled back I made sure they weren't around."

"Do you think that will work?"

"Not for long. They had a photo of you and they definitely wanted to take you in for questioning." He reached out, rubbing her shoulder in a comforting way. She wanted to lean against Jay for a minute. She needed something to break the tension riding her.

"I shouldn't need more than twenty-four hours to get this thing finished."

"Good. I'm ready to leave the dust of this island behind."

"It's such a lush paradise, it's hard to imagine corruption here."

"That's where it prospers. Don't you remember the snake in Eden?"

"Yeah. I wonder how many snakes are here."

"Someone thinks it's us. So we need to be careful."

"I always am."

As Jay parked the Jeep and they gathered their stuff to head into the hotel, Tory wished for a minute she were a different sort of girl.

Maybe she could have sought comfort in Ben's or Jay's arms tonight to forget about everything. But she knew she was too deeply private to ever allow any man access to her soul. To ever trust a man in a way that would let him know she wasn't the powerhouse she pretended to be.

She'd never really been able to trust men because she'd seen so easily that they were intimidated by a woman who knew her mind and wasn't afraid to go after what she wanted. Her father had always cautioned her to let the boys win, and when she hadn't, she'd seen her boyfriends back away. Even with Perry she sometimes sensed that their relationship would have trouble if the balance of power shifted to her at the network.

She closed her eyes for a minute, finding the quiet strength she'd always known was deep inside her. Comforting herself by looking to the future and imagining her name mentioned in the same breath as Diane Sawyer, Jane Pauley and Katie Couric.

She wondered if any of them had had to fight off rival reporters who wanted to see them fail or even land in jail. Or if they ever had to deal with handsome playboys who weren't what they seemed.

Chapter 5

Later that evening Tory walked into a tavern on the outskirts of Cabo de la Vela, one of many small mountain towns in Puerto Isla. Cabo de la Vela was only about ten miles from Paraiso, but it was a world apart. The town had a narrow, rugged road that was unpaved. The housing consisted of rough lean-tos, and there was one main street that had a restaurant with a broken Coke sign hanging over the door.

For the first time since she'd agreed to work as a courier for AA.gov, she resented having to go to a drop. Cathy Jackson had sent a research packet to Tory via overnight mail, and she'd wanted to hole up in her room to start making notes on the information Cathy had gathered.

Tory also wanted to find Shannon and tell her to back off.

She'd had a busy day of researching and writing once they'd returned from the hospital. She'd even read Thomas King's obituary. It hadn't revealed much, stating only his rank and the length of his military career and saying that he was survived by his wife, son and two brothers. She'd made two calls to Virginia but had been unable to get in touch with Ellen King, Tom's wife.

She'd called Joe Peterson at the Miami base again to find out if Ellen King knew her husband was alive. He said she'd been informed and that she wasn't talking to the media.

The bar was run-down in a pleasant way that comes from usage and not neglect. At this hour—early evening—darkness had just fallen and the bar wasn't particularly busy. Tory picked a corner table near the door but out of the main traffic flow.

There were two waitresses, and the menu consisted of some sort of fried thing that Tory's Spanish wasn't up to translating. She ordered a bottle of beer from the large-figured woman who came to take her order. She wanted to be prepared in case she needed to use the bottle as a weapon.

Maybe she should have taken the time to bring a weapon of some kind. She didn't like guns but she'd brought her hunting knife and ankle sheath with her. Her dad had taught her to use the knife when she was eight years old. Tory had always had a lot of skill with it, and practicing back at Athena had given her deadly aim.

She felt nervous and tense. Something she usually didn't associate with her courier drops, but Puerto Isla was getting to her. There was a tension in the air that said the violence of the recent coup wasn't over.

She sat in the corner waiting for her courier contact to arrive. She'd dressed carefully for this evening in a pair of black jeans, a matching undershirt and a large sapphire-blue silk shirt that she'd tucked into the jeans. The blue shirt was her signal to the person she was meeting.

A group of hikers entered the bar and took a table near the door. They were either American or European. She knew from an earlier e-mail from AA.gov that this tavern was a popular watering hole for groups of Americans who came to Puerto Isla to explore the interior mountain ranges.

The dim lighting lent the bar a feeling of ambience. She took a sip of her beer and leaned back in her chair. It had been a little over six months since she'd been in this kind of bar, a working-class place frequented by men and women after a hard day's work. This place had a real small-town meeting place feel to it, and Tory loved it.

It reminded her of the bar where her dad hung out in Placid Springs. In the back corner was a door leading to a large kitchen. Tory was tempted to go and see if they had a table set up for wives and kids back there, like Old Joe's did at home.

A child of about six or seven years ran into the bar and paused at the door. He scanned the crowd carefully. He made eye contact with her and gave her a grin that was much too charming for a child of that age.

He probably thinks I'm an easy mark for a few bucks. She reached for her wallet, intent on being the one to give the kid enough money to keep him out of bars—at least for the next few days.

"Señorita Patton?"

"*Sí.*"

He thrust a piece of paper at her before running into the kitchen. She opened the paper and found a tersely written note: "Out back five minutes."

She folded the paper and slipped it into her back pocket. Nonchalantly she glanced at her watch and took another sip of her beer.

She finished her beer, tossed a few bills on the table and stood. She walked out of the bar and paused in the shadows away from the flickering neon light.

She'd worn her hiking boots tonight because the rains had made the roads a quagmire of mud. But the boots weren't the best shoe for moving quickly to defend herself. They were heavy and awkward. She went over a few tae kwon do self-defense moves in her mind, then went on her way.

A light drizzle began to fall as she walked around the back of the building, every instinct on hyperalert. Rainy, if you're hanging around out there, watch my back.

She rounded the corner and paused to listen. She

didn't hear anything but sensed someone waiting in the dark.

"Hello?"

"Over here."

She walked toward the man's voice. There was something familiar about it. Was he the man she'd met in Paris last month? She reached into her bag and pulled out the leather pouch she'd been given in the airport in New York.

"Don't come any farther," the man said.

"Why not?" Tory wasn't used to taking orders, but on these courier gigs she'd learned that privacy and secrecy were of extreme importance.

"Put the package down and leave."

She started to obey but there was something familiar about the intonation of the man speaking. And the air of command with which he spoke. "Do I know you?"

He said nothing. She filed a few substantial facts through her mind and came up with nothing but more questions. She moved closer to the shadows. The man smelled familiar, too.

"I do….Ben?"

He cursed under his breath. A long lean hand reached out of the shadows and snagged her wrist, pulling her into the darkness with him.

She couldn't make out his expression, but she'd become intimately familiar with his body earlier this afternoon. Those same rock-hard muscles cushioned her as he tugged her deeper into the shadows.

His scent—some sort of spicy aftershave and something else that was uniquely Ben—surrounded her. This wasn't a good idea, she thought. She knew herself, knew her weaknesses too well.

"What are you doing here?"

"What are *you* doing here?"

"I asked you first," he said. "I want some answers. I thought you were a journalist here for a story. Why are you lurking around outside a dive bar in this mountain town delivering confidential packages?"

She knew then that he was more than the playboy he'd always appeared to be. And that no matter what he said, he was definitely down here doing more than checking out the local sights.

"I'm soaking up the local flavor."

He spun quickly, pinning her between his body and the hard cold concrete wall of the building. He held her jaw in an unbreakable grip, forcing her head up. Their eyes met and she didn't like what she saw in his.

"Let me go."

"Not until I have some answers."

"I'm not even sure who you are, Ben."

"Who do you work for?"

"UBC."

"Not tonight, though."

"No. Tonight I'm working for AA.gov."

"The Athena alumnae organization?"

She slid her thigh between his. He canted his hips

toward hers, and she hesitated a second too long before trying to knee him. He grunted and pressed her harder into the wall so she couldn't get leverage.

"Let me go."

"In a minute. So you're a courier and you work through AA.gov. Why you?"

"My job gives me a reason to be in hot spots without arousing suspicion."

He nodded. He let go of her jaw, drawing his fingers down her neck, where they lingered at the pulse beating hurriedly. Then he stepped away from her and leaned against the wall next to her.

"When did you start?"

"When I was in college. I knew that the military wasn't for me but I wanted to help my country."

"Idealist."

"I'm not the only one. What are you doing here? The truth this time."

He lowered his forehead so that it brushed hers. Each exhalation of his breath brushed across her face. She tried to concentrate on the questions she wanted to ask, but only one kept circling in her mind. Would he kiss her again?

Ben's lips brushed hers in a slow, sensual movement designed to seduce. But she wasn't going to be distracted from the truth tonight. She moved away from his mouth and he let her go. His hands dropped to his sides and Tory stood there in the dark, not able to hear even the sound of his breath.

"What do you want from me, Tory?" he asked in that whisper-soft tone.

It was the first time he'd said her name, and she savored the sound of it on his lips. Then she shook herself. She was in a committed relationship. This could go no further.

"Just a few answers," she said at last. The rain was soft and warm and barely penetrated the layers of her clothing.

"I can't imagine why."

"Really, Ben. I'm not falling for the I've-got-more-teeth-than-brains act anymore."

"Is that what you thought?" he asked.

He knew it was. He'd cultivated his toothy grin and charming-idiot image carefully. The man she'd met earlier in the day and again this evening was smart and savvy, two words she'd never have applied to Bennington before. "Doesn't everyone?"

"Smart-ass."

"Ah, I didn't think you'd noticed."

She could like him, and that scared her. Her relationship with Perry worked for a number of reasons—chief among them were mutual respect and affection—but beyond that they weren't all that close. They didn't laugh together or share any intimate secrets. In fact, Ben now knew more about her than Perry did.

It was a sobering thought and she shivered deep inside when she realized that she wanted to know the real man behind the different faces. She wanted to stay close to him, feeling his heat, breathing his scent and verbally sparring with him.

"What are you?" she asked.

"A man. Come closer and I'll prove it."

She backed away. She'd never been good at self-denial, and despite Perry she wanted Ben. It made perfect sense to her here in this tropical getaway, with danger at her heels, but in the real world it would be an insanity she wouldn't contemplate. "Slow down, Casanova. I had a lot of time to think."

"And?" he asked, moving closer to her.

"There's something not right about you being here. And I'm not going to rest until I figure out what it is."

He gripped her shoulders and pulled her closer to him. Her eyes had adjusted to the dark. She wished they hadn't. He looked angry.

"I thought you were on a story."

"I am. I can multitask." She shrugged, trying to free herself, but his grip was unbreakable.

"No need. Just keep your nosy self out of my business. Stop wiggling."

She couldn't back down now. She had to find out every detail of what made him tick. "That's hard."

"Why?"

"Because you're Alex's brother." If she leaned toward him their bodies would be touching.

"Believe me, Alex is happy with what she knows of me," he said.

"Ha." She had no idea why they were talking about

Alex when what she really wanted to do was not have a conversation at all.

"With comebacks like that I find it hard to believe you're a journalist."

"You make me crazy."

"Crazy good?" he asked softly, his breath brushing along the exposed curve of her neck.

"Crazy *crazy*." She tensed, waiting to see if he'd kiss her there. But she felt only the barest touch of his lips on her skin before he released her and stepped away.

"You're just plain nuts. Why are you here?"

"To interview a navy SEAL who has come back from the dead."

"If I get you your interview, will you leave me be?"

"I can't," she said honestly. If he'd been nothing more than a society playboy running through Daddy's money and supermodels, she wouldn't have even noticed him. But now that he'd shown her this other side, she couldn't let him be. He fascinated her and her curiosity was aroused along with her feminine instinct.

"Dammit, Tory. I'm not going to let some TV reporter ruin this."

"Ruin what?"

"Nothing. If you want your interview with Tom King, you better forget you ever saw me here. Where's my package?" he asked. Why was he so angry? It wasn't as if she was going to go on network television and expose him as a...what the heck was he?

She thrust the leather pouch to him. She'd forgotten she still had it in her hands. "Why are you so angry?"

"Because you can't forget your damned job long enough to do what's right."

She realized he'd misunderstood her. "I wouldn't—"

"Go back to your hotel and wait for the call. You'll have your interview with King in the next twelve hours. But I'm serious, Tory. Cross me on this and you'll regret it."

He pivoted on his heel and walked away before she could respond. She watched him leave. Rubbing her arms, she wondered how a few innocent questions had turned into the inquisition.

Tory exited the alley muttering to herself about stubborn, hardheaded men. Since she was just as determined about her job, she could understand why he'd taken the hard line. But at the same time he should know her reputation well enough to realize she didn't do stories that would hurt anyone who didn't deserve it. And it seemed that a story on Ben would blow his cover and make it impossible for him to function.

Did he think she was one of those bimbos he usually dated? She didn't care what he thought. After tonight it was doubtful she'd see him again.

She heard footsteps behind her. She stopped and turned, expecting to see Bennington Forsythe, but no one was there. Creeped out, she started walking again, this time at a quicker pace. She hugged her purse to her side and then realized she was advertising the fact that she wanted to be a victim.

She straightened her spine. There was nothing out here in the night that she couldn't take on. She'd been tested and had proved herself many times in battle. Repeating her mantra—it's hard to defeat an enemy with outposts in your head—she continued toward the Jeep.

She had one more deserted shop front to walk past and then she'd be safely back in that rickety old Jeep. Actually she was probably in a better place out here. The pocket of darkness made her wary, and she hurried her pace again but then stopped.

Someone was in the shadows.

"Ben?"

The red-hot glow of a cigar flashed and the pungent scent assailed her. She turned to cross the street and found a man behind her. He wore grubby jeans, a sleeveless T-shirt and a straw cowboy hat that had seen better days.

The rain still fell in a steady drizzle. Tory cursed her luck. The man with the cigar moved out from the shadows. He had a long scar that ran the length of his face from his temple to his jaw. He was taller than she was and about two hundred pounds heavier.

"You will come with us," he said in broken English.

"No, thanks." Tory edged away from the two men.

Scarface laughed. The sound sent chills down her spine. "You misunderstand, Miss Patton. It wasn't an invitation."

They knew who she was. At first that scared her. Was it another of Shannon's schemes to make sure that Tory didn't get her story, or something more sinister? Or maybe they were a rebel group who needed media coverage.

"What do you want from me?"

"Grab her, Jose," the man said in Spanish, probably not knowing that she spoke the language.

Jose stepped closer, and Tory feinted to the right and tried to dash around him. But the man was smarter than he looked and grabbed her around the middle. He brought his free hand up to her throat and held her with her neck tipped back. Her purse dropped from her hand.

He tightened his grasp until she fought for every breath. And got pissed off. Her pulse quickened as she grabbed his wrist in both hands. Dropping her body weight forward, she flipped him over her shoulder. She backed away and brought her hands up in a defensive pose.

He got up unsteadily and charged straight at her. He hit her with a punch to the stomach, followed by a jab toward her face. Tory doubled over before he made contact with her nose.

The man with the cigar circled around behind her and Tory knew she couldn't fight two men at once. She gasped for breath and remembered a bit of advice her tae kwon do instructor had offered her long ago. In a street fight, go for the legs and take your opponent down.

She aimed a side kick at Jose's leg just above the knee and watched his leg crumple. She spun and kicked out again, this time catching him in the ribs. She aimed just below the ninth rib and knew she'd hit her target when he fell to the ground. Tory was sure she'd knocked him out. Whirling quickly, she faced Jose's accomplice.

"Very nice, Miss Patton," Scarface said.

"I cherish your praise."

He stubbed out his cigar on his forearm and placed it in his pocket. Tory backed away to keep both men in her line of vision. Jose hadn't moved since she'd kicked him. But she wasn't taking chances.

Instead of waiting for Scarface to attack, she went on the offensive. She took a deep breath and centered herself. Lashed out with a spinning hook kick to Scarface's hamstrings. She spun away and fell back into a fighting stance. The kick should have rendered one of his legs useless, but he moved back and the kick didn't hit him squarely.

She caught him under the chin with a knife-hand blow to his neck. His head snapped back. Tory danced away and came back with a high kick to his head. He leaned back and grabbed her foot to yank her off balance. Tory used his hold on her foot as a weight. She hooked her other leg around his knees and leaned forward, forcing him to let go of her ankle as they both went down.

She rolled and sprang to her feet again. Her ankle

throbbed, dammit. Scarface stayed down. The fall had knocked him out. She grabbed her purse and sprinted to her vehicle, digging for the keys. She got inside the Jeep and started it.

Her hands were shaking and her ankle throbbed. She wasn't GI Jane. She was a relatively successful urban girl with some martial-arts training who was out of her environment. She struggled not to let panic set in as she drove away.

The road was a patchwork of muddy potholes, which forced Tory to concentrate on driving. Slowly the adrenaline from her encounter seeped away.

An American journalist was just the kind of political hostage some of the gunrunners or drug dealers could use. But if those men were criminals, why hadn't they been armed?

Chapter 6

Jay was waiting inside the hotel for her when she returned. Though it was only a little after eight it felt more like midnight. He took one look at the way she was hobbling and steered her into the bar for a shot of tequila.

He handed her the shot glass and Tory took it thankfully, swallowing the liquor in one gulp.

She leaned back against the wooden chair and closed her eyes. She heard a chair scrape backward, and then Jay sat down across from her.

"Making friends again?" he asked. He pulled out a cigar and a clipper. Trimming the end of it, he rolled it through his fingers a few times, then brought it to his mouth and lit the end.

She forced a smile. She was getting edgy, and the feeling of everything going to crap was getting stronger. This wasn't the first time she'd had a difficult time getting a story, but it was the first time that so many different elements in her life had converged. "You know me. Always the life of the party."

"Actually, Tory, you are."

She enjoyed a reputation not only as a brilliant journalist but also as a very good-natured woman. "I know. Obviously the natives don't realize how likable I am."

"Obviously. What happened?" he asked.

She debated how much to tell Jay. He'd become her father confessor since she'd been here. She didn't like leaning on him, but without Perry she had no one to talk to here. "A couple of guys tried to grab me."

"Rape?"

"I don't think so. They knew my name and wanted me to come with them."

"Probably a group of drug or gunrunners. The new regime frowns on that kind of activity, so having a pretty American journalist as a hostage could be very beneficial to them."

"That's one theory. But the sentiment in the city is very pro-coca ranchers from what I heard when I talked to the people in the marketplace, so I'm not too sure that was their goal," she said.

"What were you doing tonight?"

"A little person-to-person research." She couldn't let Jay know that she was a courier for the government.

He raised one eyebrow, waiting for her to continue. She realized she had to come up with something. "What about Shannon?"

"I saw her earlier talking to an older man. I think he works for Perez's office."

"I wonder if she's filed a story yet. I'm going to call Perry and find out."

"How's things with Perry?"

"Fine. Why do you ask?"

"For the same reason I always do," he said after a moment.

Jay had made no secret of the fact that he wanted to see her. Or at least see her naked. But she had to wonder if maybe he'd picked up on some of her restlessness with that relationship. Regardless, she wasn't ready to make a change, and certainly not without talking to Perry first. "Things are fine. Back to Shannon— do you think she would have sent those guys tonight?"

"It's possible, given the nature of the rumor she started, that they may have believed you were a contact for them."

Tory took her glass from the bartender and sipped at this one. She was too tired to really think straight. Pulling out one of her notepads, she wrote down a few notes. "We forgot one."

"What?"

"Maybe they wanted me to interview their leader."

"A possibility."

She added that to her notes and then jotted down descriptions of both men. She thought there might be a story in this somewhere. Gathering her stuff and herself, she stood. She wanted to ice her ankle and rest.

"Thanks for the drink," she said.

"No problem. I've been trying a convince you to have a drink with me for a long time."

"Not tonight, Jay."

He set his cigar on the table and reached for her hands. "Why not? You look like you could use a shoulder to lean on."

She was conflicted and couldn't deal with thoughts of Jay tonight. He tempted her, but then he always had because he was fun. But she was still involved with Perry.

"I can't," she said with what she hoped was finality. She nodded her goodbye and walked away.

The night clerk at the desk looked up as she approached the elevator.

"Tory Patton?"

"Yes."

"I have a message for you."

She crossed to him. He dug around on his desk and finally located an envelope with her name on it. He handed it to her. She took some money from her pocket and gave it to the man.

"Thanks."

She pushed the envelope into her pocket as she waited for the elevator to arrive. Finally she was in her room. She tossed her bag on the bed and pulled off her torn shirt.

She bent and removed her boots and gently probed her ankle. It wasn't swelling, but a bruise was starting to form. She'd wrap it before she went back out.

Pulling the envelope from her pocket, she used her nail to rip it open. A slip of paper fell out.

Come to the Vista Del Mar Hotel in Paraiso if you want to meet King.

Tory sat up straight, her fatigue falling away as she realized her interview was at hand. She stripped out of her clothing, which was dirty from her earlier altercation, and took a quick shower. Ten minutes later she was on her way down the hall toward the lobby. Her wet hair clung to the back of her neck.

She'd packed up everything in her room and brought it downstairs with her. Jay was in the lobby speaking to a local when she returned.

"Grab your camera and come on."

He said something to the man he'd been talking to and followed her. Ten minutes later they were on their way to the Vista Del Mar and Tom King.

Jay drove so she could review her interview questions and notes one more time. She jotted a few final questions on her notepad as they neared the hotel. Jay followed her directions to the parking lot.

King was in the hotel and no longer at the hospital—and Ben had something to do with that. It was a circumstance she planned to explore when she got inside. It was a few minutes after nine when they got out of the car.

"What are we doing here?"

"I got a tip that King was here."

"From who? This could be a trap."

Tory knew that the note had come from Ben, but knew he wouldn't want Jay to know. "It's reliable."

"It's not just your ass if turns out to be Perez's idea of a joke."

"Perez won't give me the time of day. You're going to have to trust me, Jay."

He looked at her for a long minute, then turned and gathered his equipment. Tory helped him by carrying in the sound equipment. It wouldn't be the first time she'd miked herself and the person she was interviewing.

The hotel lobby wasn't as run-down as the place they were staying in. When they entered, a man in jeans and a dark T-shirt stopped them. His carriage had an air of military to it.

"Tory Patton?"

"Yes."

"I'm Robert O'Neill. Follow me."

"Who are you with, Robert?"

"The military," he said, which wasn't much of an answer. Which branch? Why wasn't he in uniform?

She didn't have a chance to ask him any other questions. He led them to the second floor and into a suite with a sitting room. The room to the connecting suite was ajar.

"I'll set up over there," Jay said.

Tory nodded. "I need to change and then I'll come back and help you set up." She turned to O'Neill. "Is Thomas King here yet?"

"He'll be here in a moment, Ms. Patton. You can use that room to change," he said, gesturing to the right.

Tory took her garment bag and entered the small bathroom. She changed quickly and applied her makeup with a heavy hand, knowing that the lights would wash her out if she didn't. She smiled reassuringly at herself in the mirror and practiced a few of her questions.

She closed the lid on the toilet seat and sat down, adjusted the buttons on her jacket and then stood and sat down again. Her clothing was free of constrictions and she felt comfortable.

She left her jeans and T-shirt folded on the counter and reentered the room. Only Jay was there and he had the lights set up and was loading the tape in the beta camera.

Tory looked at the chairs and then rearranged the angle of each one. "How's this?"

They discussed the placement of the chairs, and Tory moved from one to the other so that Jay could check the camera angles.

The door to the connecting suite opened and a tall, gaunt man walked in. Tory closed her eyes for a minute to compose herself. She'd expected him to look bad, but the reality was so much worse. He had a jagged scar on his neck and a bandage over his left temple, and he looked as if he might weigh less than she did. His clothes hung from his body like rags on a scarecrow.

She opened her eyes again and met his green-gold gaze. In his expression she saw determination and a quiet kind of rage. She sensed that, though his body was temporarily not up to fighting, his spirit was. His blond hair was thick but cut short and neat.

"I'm Tory Patton with UBC. Thank you for granting me this interview," she said, holding out her hand.

He took her hand and shook it. She noticed that despite his gaunt appearance he had a strong grip and his hands were warm. "You're welcome, Ms. Patton. Please call me Tom."

"I'm going to have to mike you," she said.

Once he was back in shape he'd be a very attractive man. His eyes were fatigued and his body battered but his charisma shone through.

Tory smiled back at him. She had him loosen his shirt so they could wire him with the microphone. Then they were ready.

"What's your rank, Tom?" she asked, to establish him in the eyes of her audience.

"I'm a commander in the U.S. Navy."

"Take us through your mission from the beginning," Tory said.

"I came down with a platoon on a leader recon mission."

"What is leader recon?"

"My team was assessing the situation. We verified that hostages were being held in one of the small mountain towns on the west side of the island."

"Americans?"

"Yes, from Doctors without Borders. The dossier we received said there were three men and one woman."

"What happened next?"

"We verified the location of the hostages and then we went in to extricate them. We were ambushed by the previous government's military."

"How?" she asked. A hundred new questions popped up. SEAL teams were elite. No one knew when a platoon was deployed or where it was going. How would the old government have the knowledge that the team was coming in?

"We entered the compound and found the hostages had already been executed. As soon as our team was inside, they opened fire on us. We returned fire but were outnumbered."

"Take me through the last moments when you saw your crew alive."

Tom gave her a look that would have scorched steel, but Tory didn't flinch. Her questions had to be probing and go past the superficial. She needed to know what he'd felt—that's what viewers tuned in to see.

"We were under heavy fire. I ordered my team to retreat. A bullet grazed my temple and I lost consciousness. When I woke up I was in prison."

"What did they want from you?" she asked, knowing he'd been tortured.

"They asked me repeatedly about my mission and how long we'd been on Puerto Isla before we took action."

She asked him several questions about his imprisonment and listened to him detail the torture he'd endured while his captors tried to find out more details of his mission. Tom had refused to tell them anything.

She swallowed against the tears burning at the back of her eyes. This man had sacrificed so much for his country, and she felt proud to be sitting across from him. And infinitely saddened that he'd lost his friends and teammates. More questions formed in the back of her mind.

She needed to do some digging. It made no sense that the government would know the SEALs were coming, and clearly it had. Santiago had been anti-American, and the U.S. wouldn't have given him any information.

"How were you found and rescued?"

"I was able to bribe one of my jailers to send a message to the U.S. Embassy."

"Then you were freed by Del Torro's government?"

"Yes."

"Tell me what happened."

"I was taken to the hospital and my wounds were treated."

"And then you were moved here to the hotel?"

"Yes, ma'am."

"Why?"

"I'm not at liberty to say."

Tory let it drop for now.

"One last question, Tom. What is the one thing you want to do now that you're out of captivity?"

"Kiss my wife."

Tory left Jay packing up his equipment and changed back into her jeans. She wasn't ready to head back to her hotel. Something wasn't right with Tom King's story. No one should have known that the SEALs were coming and from what he'd said, some-one had.

She was going to get some answers from Juan Perez's office if she had to camp on his steps all day long.

"Ready, Tory?" Jay asked.

"I want to hear more about what the city was like earlier this year when the SEAL team came in. I'm going to talk to the military men who are here. Can you hang around a few hours?"

Tory had the feeling it wouldn't be long before history started to repeat itself on Puerto Isla. Despite its tropical beauty, there wasn't enough of a tourist trade to keep the economy going without illegal activities.

"Sure."

"I'm going to go down to the lobby and see what I can get from the bar crowd."

"Keep an eye out for Shannon. I don't think she followed us here, but you can never be too sure."

"I will. Where will you be?"

"I want to talk to our friend Robert O'Neill and then I'm going to call Perez again. I don't want him to know we spoke to King yet."

Jay left and she went into the bathroom to gather the rest of her stuff. When she came back into the main hotel room, Robert was waiting for her. "I'll make sure you get back to your car safely."

"I'm not ready to leave yet. Would you mind answering a few questions for me, Robert?"

"Depends on the questions."

"How did you get involved with King?" Tom had refused to answer any questions about how he'd come to be at the hotel. In fact, after the interview he'd been hustled out of the room they'd used and moved to an undisclosed location. She had warned the men with him that Shannon might be following her and that the local police were also watching her. She figured the team that had busted King out of prison was probably a very elite military group that didn't want or need any publicity. And she understood that.

"I can't say."

"Are you part of a Special Forces team?"

She was also trying to figure out how Bennington Forsythe fit into the picture. Because she knew that Ben had something to do with Tom King and the rescue.

She just couldn't believe the conclusions she drew on her own. She needed more information.

He nodded, but refused to answer any more of her questions. In fact, he opened the door leading to the hallway, checked the hall and then took her elbow, leading her out of the room.

"What branch of the military are you with?" she asked as he led her to the stairwell and started down the steps.

"Does it matter?" he asked over his shoulder.

It did, but he obviously wasn't going to tell her. She tried a different angle. "How many men are here with you?" she asked. She'd heard voices in the other suite while they'd been cleaning up after the interview. There had been at least two, maybe three men in that other room besides Tom King. If Robert didn't come through with some answers, she'd double back and do some investigating on her own.

He paused on the landing and faced her. "You talk a lot, don't you, lady?"

She grinned at him. "Yes, I do. It's part of my appeal."

"Don't count on it," said a voice behind her.

She turned and saw Ben at the top of the stairs. Where had he come from? Dressed in faded jeans and a T-shirt that clung to his chest, Ben leaned in the doorway. "I thought we had a deal."

"What kind of deal?" she asked. She was not flirting with him, she assured herself. Her questions were for the greater good. He was a puzzle and she had to figure him out.

"I get you your interview, you leave me alone," he said, crossing his arms over his chest.

"I don't recall those stipulations," Tory said.

He shrugged and looked past her. "I'll take care of Ms. Patton, Robert."

"Yes, sir."

Robert walked past her without another word. She waited until he was gone before looking back at Ben. "What are you doing here?"

"You keep asking me that," he said, taking her arm and leading her down the stairs.

"I'm going to keep on asking until you give me an answer."

"Why?" he asked.

"Why what?" she countered. Playing games wasn't normally her style, but there was something about Ben that made her contrary.

She shook her head. Felt the weight of her hair brush her cheek and reached up to tuck the strand behind her ear only to encounter Ben's hand. He pushed her hair back, and his callused fingers rubbed the rim of her ear. She shivered.

"I'm not going to let you distract me, Ben. I need to get to the bottom of this."

"Not here," he said, and led her out of the stairwell and into a room on another floor.

And then they were totally alone.

Chapter 7

The room Ben took her to was decorated in the same bland style as the one in which she'd interviewed Tom King. There was a duffel bag on the end of the bed next to a neat pile of clothing. The light was on in the bathroom. She noted the pile of wet towels on the floor and the damp shower curtain pushed to one side. There was a shaving kit on the counter.

It was almost ten-thirty now and she wondered if Ben and his men were going to try to move King tonight. She knew then that if they were, she was going to be there. She'd have to phone Jay and have him bring the Jeep around back.

Ben turned on the television.

"I was serious about the questions, Ben. I don't

want to watch TV." She had a feeling he thought he could placate her with a few platitudes and some double-talk.

"I know. I'm using it to cover the sound of our conversation."

"Oh." She hadn't thought of that. But then she wasn't usually trying to keep people from overhearing her conversations. To cover her awkwardness she pulled out her notepad and pen.

"This is strictly off the record, Tory. Understand?" he asked. His steely-eyed gaze reminded her of his lethal efficiency at the hospital when he'd gotten them out of the heavily patrolled facility.

"Yes. I know what that means. I'm just making notes so that I can figure out what's going on with King."

Still he hesitated, and Tory knew she had to put him at ease. This wasn't an interview, but she needed more of the facts to put the pieces of the story into perspective.

"I never thanked you," she said quietly. If Ben hadn't interceded, she'd still be chasing her tail and trying to outwit Perez and the Puerto Isla policemen.

He leaned back against the dresser and crossed his arms over his chest. Muscles bulged in his arms. Why was she noticing this now? Perry had nice muscles, she reminded herself.

"For getting you to King?" he asked.

She nodded.

"You're welcome," he said at last.

"I don't understand what's going on. The Del Torro

government invited me down here," she said, when it became apparent he wasn't going to add anything else.

"Who did?" Ben asked.

She realized he was making notes as she was, but instead of writing them down he was keeping it all in his head. That fit with what she knew of Alex's brother. Though he had earned a reputation for a playboy, he'd also graduated with top honors from a military prep school and college.

"Juan Perez," she said. "The minister of foreign affairs."

"That makes sense. Take me through everything that happened once you arrived," he ordered.

"I'm asking the questions here."

"Humor me."

But he didn't look as if he was joking and so far he hadn't given her any information that she could use. "I'm not sure you have much of a sense of humor."

"Okay, smart-ass, you made your point. But I'm in charge of getting King off Puerto Isla alive. I need all the information you have."

"I'll tell you what I know, but I want to follow you out with him. Kind of a look inside the rescue."

"Can't do it. My team is top secret."

"I won't film it."

"We can negotiate that later," he said.

He didn't intend to let her go with him. But she knew how to follow a story and had been called tenacious as a pit bull by one upset merchant on whom

she'd done an exposé. In the end the public had bene-
fited from her story. And she sensed that the public
should know what was going on down here, whether
she could give them all the details or not.

"What are you doing here? And why is King at the
hotel and no longer in the hospital?" she asked, changing gears.

"He was no longer safe."

"From the Puerto Isla government?" Tory wasn't
sure she was following this. Why would Tom King no
longer be safe? His rescue and freedom was the kind
of public-relations stunt that newly formed governments seldom got. Returning King to the U.S. was a
huge goodwill gesture from a country that had been
under trade embargoes for a long time.

"Yes. When I ran into you at the hospital, I overheard two of the doctors talking about sedating King
so that he could be moved to another location. I know
for certain that the U.S. was not in on that decision."

"What is going on here? First Perez and the navy
call me down here for an interview, then things go to
hell."

"You're the wild card in all this." He rubbed his
chin and then straightened from the door, walking toward her.

Tory held her ground. "Do you think it has something to do with me and King?"

"Is there a connection between you two?"

"Not beyond this story."

"I didn't think so. My intel didn't mention you."

His pager went off and he glanced at the screen. "I've got to pack up."

"I'm not done asking questions," she said, barring his way into the bathroom.

"Patton, I'm on a short clock."

"Then let me help you. I have a lot of information on King, and something doesn't add up about his capture."

"That's not my problem."

"I can be a real pain in the ass."

He laughed. "I like you, Tory Patton."

She liked him, too. That was the real problem. She couldn't afford the kind of distraction that Ben provided. He pressed closer to her and she stood her ground. But when she tipped her head back to meet his gaze, he lowered his mouth to hers.

She closed her eyes, forgetting about the story and the complications this could bring. Forgetting about Perry and the fact that she was in a serious relationship. It was only the tension of feeling that she was going to die. The danger of being on this island where everything kept changing. If she'd learned anything from her time in the 24/7 world of television news, she'd learned that nothing lasted forever.

And you were only given opportunities once in a lifetime.

A loud explosion rocked the floor and she barely kept her balance. She cried out and Ben's strong grip helped keep her upright. Immediately the distinctive beeping of Ben's pager began again and he pulled back and glanced at the message screen again. This time he left her to go to the phone. He had a short conversation. Tory used the time to call Jay and alert him that they might be moving soon.

"What's going on?" she asked when Ben hung up.

"Someone tried to kill Tom King." Ben's voice was low pitched, his words spoken without emotion.

"Is he okay?" Tory asked. It didn't seem fair that he should survive a brutal ambush and torture in prison only to die once he was supposedly safe.

"Yes. I'm getting him out of here tonight," Ben said.

"You mean your team, right?"

"Yes. We're taking him to meet a chopper at an unused airstrip on the outskirts of town."

"Won't that be dangerous?" she asked. From what she'd observed of Puerto Isla since she'd arrived here, once you left Paraiso the natives weren't exactly friendly.

"Who's the expert here?" he asked, sounding pissed off.

She went to his side and put her hand on his arm. She wished she knew what he was thinking. "Don't get offended. Are you an expert?"

"I knew you couldn't keep from asking questions."

"Stop evading them. I'm not going to turn your life into an exposé. I do understand that if you are what I'm beginning to believe you are, then your public image is sacrosanct."

"Thanks, I think."

"What are you?"

He sighed, then seemed to come to a decision. "I'm part of an elite fighting force known as LASER. Lost Airmen's Service. We rescue military personnel who have been captured."

"And your playboy lifestyle enables you to travel around the world without suspicion."

"Except when I'm encountering my little sister's friends."

She knew precious little about him as a man. He'd always seemed so frivolous and not worth her time. But now that she'd seen the keen intelligence gleaming in his eyes, seen him in action in dangerous circumstances and in intimate ones…she wanted to know more.

"I know you're in a hurry. What should I do?"

"Get your gear together."

Tory gathered her stuff and was ready when Ben opened the door leading into the hall. He pulled his gun from his holster and swept the area before grabbing her wrist and leading her out of the room. She twisted out of his grasp. He didn't even break stride.

"I'll have Robert take you back to your hotel," he said, leading her down the hall to the room where she'd interviewed Tom earlier.

"That's okay. Jay's downstairs waiting for me."

"Who's Jay?"

"My cameraman."

For a moment she felt a twinge of embarrassment

as he opened the door and five guys looked up. Tom King smiled at her. Robert gave her a frown and the others appeared mildly curious. One of the men had a wounded arm and another guy—Tory assumed he was a medic—was bandaging him up.

"What happened?"

"Someone fired a rocket-propelled grenade into the three rooms we rented on this floor."

"How did they know where we were?" Ben asked.

Robert looked straight at Tory. "I'm not sure. But Ms. Patton and her cameraman went up and down the elevator several times."

"I'm sorry. I didn't realize the location was secretive."

"I should have told you," Ben said. "This one's on my shoulders."

As Tory listened to Ben, she was surprised to realize that he wasn't just part of a military group, but the leader of one. The men's attitudes as they listened and spoke with Ben showed that they respected him. Tory filed away this new piece of information.

"I'm going to have to ask you to leave," Ben said.

Tory nodded and eased her way out of the room. She stayed in the hallway. She called Jay and told him to move the Jeep around to the back. "Be ready to move. Did you see any more police?"

"No, but Shannon showed up right before you called. She knows something's going on here."

"Okay, I'm waiting outside the hotel room to see if

I can get any more information. I might need the hidden camera again."

"I'll get it ready for you. And Tory?"

"Yes, Jay?"

"Be careful."

The door opened behind her. "I've got to go."

She disconnected the call. Jay's concern touched her. She knew she could count on him and his friendship.

"What are you still doing here?" Ben asked.

"Let me go with you, Ben."

"No. This isn't something fit for network news. We're talking life and death here."

"I won't endanger you or King. I'm an Athena grad. You know they train us how to survive."

"I don't care how much training you've had. I don't want anything to happen to you."

"I can take care of myself."

"Tory...."

"Give me a break, Ben. If that's your only objection, stuff it."

"Dammit, woman. I take care of my own."

"I'm not yours."

He swore under his breath and turned away from her.

She knew she'd pushed him, but she didn't like men telling her what to do. She wasn't some eighteen-year-old kid who'd never faced a challenge in her life. She'd been trained to use her wits in tough situations. The entire affair with Tom King was right up her alley. Tory viewed it the same way she would a courier assignment for AA.gov.

"I think I can be of assistance or I wouldn't have suggested this."

Ben leaned his head against the wall and she sensed he was running through his options. She stayed silent.

"You can come with us to the airstrip, but that's it. King needs to be debriefed before he talks to any more reporters."

"Okay."

Tory shrugged into her backpack and followed the men. No one was waiting for the elevator, but Ben bypassed the car for the stairs. Robert had done the same thing. She knew it was to avoid walking into a trap.

If she hadn't seen him in action before, she probably would be staring open-mouthed at him now. It was such a change from the man she'd known since she was a fourteen-year-old girl. This guy hardly resembled Alex's brother as she'd always known him.

The group moved quickly down the stairs to the lobby. Tory saw Jay standing off to one side. He had the tapes and her laptop, and they'd meet in Miami. He met her eyes and she nodded to him to follow the team of U.S. soldiers. A group of Puerto Isla's police was at the front desk. Probably to investigate the explosion.

"Robert, you take the decoy team straight through the lobby and out the front door. We'll rendezvous in

Miami. King and I will go out the back. You—" he pointed to Tory "—follow me."

And Tory followed Ben and Tom out the back door and into the tropical night.

Chapter 8

They left the hotel via a back entrance through the kitchen. Tory was glad she hadn't eaten any meals at the hotel when she saw the state of the kitchen.

"No wonder I have heartburn," Tom said.

"Didn't hear you complaining when you were scarfing down the food."

"Hey, it had been a long time between meals," Tom said.

Tory realized that though the men had never met before this mission they shared a camaraderie that she didn't understand. There was an excited air of energy around both of them. They were a walking army with all the weaponry they had on their persons.

They were similarly dressed in green jungle camouflage. Tory wore a pair of khaki pants and a black T-shirt. Her hiking boots were top quality, and she had a feeling they'd have a chance to prove their durability before she got back home.

"Tory, get between Tom and me. I'll go first. When I signal you, come on."

"Okay," she said.

"What, no questions?" he asked, with that wise-ass grin of his.

Tom might have been half starved, but he still moved with the ease of a trained tiger.

She wanted to talk to Tom in more detail about his mission. Could he have witnessed something that he wasn't aware of? Why was someone trying to kill a man who'd been in prison for the past six months?

Both men were armed with standard military-issue handguns. Ben hadn't offered her a piece and she was glad. She knew she didn't have enough skill to kill with one. But she did have her knife. Quickly she removed it from her backpack along with the ankle sheath. She lifted her pant leg and fastened it on. Finally Ben got a signal on his wireless earpiece. "We're moving out."

She waited for Ben to move first. He slipped out the back door. Tory waited for him to signal her. Tom stood close behind her, covering Ben from the doorway.

She recognized that Tom didn't like taking orders. He took them, but he was used to being in command. It was an interesting observation and she tucked it away for later. She hoped he'd agree to a follow-up interview once they were back in the States.

Seconds later Ben signaled her. Tory moved into the shadows as soundlessly as she could. Skills she'd mastered when she'd been at Athena came to the fore. Once again, she called on Rainy's presence and felt a little better because her friend was in her head with her.

The smell of rotting trash mixed with the warm sea breeze. She remembered her lessons and slowed her breathing.

She moved cautiously across the alley and then stood behind Ben as he surveyed the open area. Tom joined them.

The LASER team had two Jeeps. One was parked two blocks from the hotel in an abandoned garage. The three of them were to make their way to that vehicle.

"Something doesn't feel right," Tom said.

"Yeah, but what?"

"I don't know."

"Tory, go to ground behind that trash can."

She didn't argue, just slipped away from the men and crouched behind the large trash container. She took her knife from the sheath at her ankle and waited. Tom covered Ben as he stepped into the mouth of the alley. Ben surveyed the area and then motioned for them to come forward.

Before Tory could move from her spot all hell broke loose. Ben and Tom were facing four rough-looking men with submachine guns and nasty attitudes.

Tory shrank back against the wall as a flashlight played over the alley. They were saying something to Ben, but Tory couldn't make out the words. The men took the guns from both Tom and Ben and forced them to their knees. Tory knew she'd have only a second to make her move. When the leader raised his gun and pointed it at Ben's head, she drew back her arm and let her blade fly with deadly accuracy.

Ben and Tom both attacked when the man fell. Tory ran down the alleyway. Her hands were trembling, but she focused on the job at hand. She raced at another man and hit him with a surprise roundhouse kick to the neck. He staggered and she brought her other leg around in a hook kick. She caught him behind the knees, and he fell to the ground.

She gave him a short punch to the jaw. His head snapped back. And then she finished him with a side chop to the neck. She put her foot on the small of his back, unsure what to do with him now that he was unconscious.

"Catch," Ben said.

She glanced up in time to see a pair of plastic handcuffs coming at her. She grabbed them and bound his wrists. She stood up and clenched her fingers together. She needed her knife back.

Ben grabbed the guy she'd taken down under the shoulders and dragged him back in the alley where Tom had taken the other two. The fourth man was dead. She started toward him only to stop.

"I've got it, Tory. Get over there with Tom."

Now that the moment of danger had passed, she felt a fine trembling start deep inside. She'd never been in a situation quite like this before. Sure, the women's prison had been scary when she'd gone undercover there. And Scarface and Jose had been a shock. But she'd known deep inside in both cases that she wasn't going to die.

Ben retrieved her knife and moved the dead body out of the open area and into the shadows. Tory was shaking so hard now that she wasn't sure she could continue on with this. Maybe she should go back to her hotel room. But at the same time, a part of her knew that if she hadn't been there, both Ben and Tom would be dead.

"Athena women can do anything." Rainy had said that to Tory more than once when Tory had called for advice from her mentor.

Tom held his M-9 in a steady grip. He had one of the submachine guns slung over his shoulder along with an extra ammunition clip. Tory bent down and picked up one of the other guns. It was beginning to look as if they'd need an arsenal to get off the island in one piece.

Tom patted her awkwardly on the shoulder. Tory couldn't even mutter her thanks to him. Oh, my God, she thought, I'm going to be sick. She swallowed several times and then realized she was breathing too quickly. She closed her eyes, but all she could see was the fallen man. She'd taken a life. Another person's life. Something she'd never been prepared to do.

Ben joined them, squeezed her hand and then handed her the knife. The blade had been cleaned. She bent and replaced it in the sheath at her ankle.

"There weren't that many exits out of the hotel. They were probably watching them all," Tom said.

"Nice job, Patton," Ben said, his eagle eyes on her.

She straightened, took a deep breath. She had to show him that she could stay with them. "I am an Athena grad, Ben. We can take care of ourselves." Apart from the fact that she was this close to puking. She hoped she'd kept the tremors out of her voice. She knew he was looking for a reason to leave her behind.

"Good thing," Tom said.

Ben stooped and picked up the remaining man's gun and searched the bodies for extra ammunition.

"What the hell does Tom know that they are willing to kill for?" Tory asked.

"Search me," Tom said with a grimace.

"I think they already did that," Ben said. He turned to her. "Thanks for saving our asses."

"No problem."

"Let's move out," Tom said. "Obviously someone already knows the decoy isn't me and they're determined not to let us get away."

"In a minute," Ben said. He turned to Tory. "You okay?"

She nodded. She couldn't talk anymore. She just

couldn't do it. She needed to gather her thoughts and figure out how to keep both men from guessing what was going on with her.

"Ever killed a man before?" Ben asked.

She shook her head.

"Come here." He pulled her into his arms, rubbing his big hands up and down her back. The chills started to recede, and in a minute she stopped shaking and pushed herself away from him.

He gave her the once-over and then nodded. "Let's go."

"Should we be seen with all these weapons?"

"I'm not walking into another situation like this one."

Tom nodded his agreement. "Can you handle that gun?"

"I fired one for a piece I did on illegal guns on the street. Street gangs in L.A. A lot of them used guns like this one."

Dawn was breaking over the horizon. The beach was a few streets over, and the sidewalks were lined with palm trees and tropical plants. The dichotomy of the tropical-paradise foliage and the life-threatening situation made her want to laugh. She knew it was nerves and forced herself to breathe deeply.

Ben took the lead again, and this time she noticed he didn't seem reluctant to have her along. She still felt shaky inside and hoped they could get off the island without further incident. But she knew if they didn't, she'd do what needed to be done.

"Wait here."

The garage was run-down like most of the buildings on the outskirts of Paraiso, but the windows were still in place and at some time in the not so distant past someone had whitewashed the walls. Ben disappeared inside.

Tom stood ready, tension in every line of his body. Tory mirrored his readiness, determined to be prepared for whatever came next.

"Well, hell," Ben said, his voice carrying over to them. Tom pushed past her and entered the car bay. The hood of the Jeep was up, and the engine lay in pieces on the floor around the vehicle.

"Either of you know how to reassemble an engine?" Ben asked. He crouched next to the engine parts and picked up two of them.

"I don't," Tom said.

"Me, either, but I can call and get someone at the network to talk us through it," Tory said.

Ben pushed to his feet and pulled his Colt .45 from the holster and checked the magazine. "Forget it. It's time to drop back to Plan B. We'll go on foot. Tom, can you walk about fifteen miles?" Ben asked.

The older man paused in his search of the back seat of the Jeep. He was loading a standard-issue backpack with the rations and water that had been stored there just in case. "Yes."

"Good, let's move out. We need to get out of the city and into the jungle area before people start moving around."

They said little as they worked their way through the city streets that were just now waking up. Tory was aware of an energy buzzing through her veins that felt not unlike the kind of high reporting usually gave her.

Tory knew that something was changing deep inside her. For the first time in her life she was out of her element. It was an odd feeling, and she didn't like it. Because she never could tolerate being out of control.

The interior of Puerto Isla was a dense jungle terrain that she knew, from a trip to Brazil the previous summer, made the Amazon rain forest feel like a nice day at the spa. Tory was drenched in sweat before noon. Ben moved as if he was accustomed to the damp heat. A dark sweat stain appeared between his shoulder blades. She stared at his back as she walked, her mind alive with images of him from last night.

His black pants pulled tight across his backside with each step he took. His arm lifted high to slash hanging vines out of their path with a machete he'd produced from his pack.

"Anyone need a break?" Ben asked over his shoulder. They'd been walking for about two hours. Ben had estimated they would reach the airport the following day. The jungle growth was dense and thick, slowing their progress.

He noticed where her gaze was and quirked one eyebrow. She shrugged at him. What could she say? The man was worth staring at and she suspected he knew it.

"I'm fine," Tom said.

"Me, too," Tory said, taking a sip from her water bottle. Despite being so sweaty, she was enjoying herself.

"Aren't you a little old for active command, Tom?" Tory asked. The question had been bugging her. He was forty-five, and she knew today's military was trying to be more politically correct, but young tough guys were usually who they wanted on the front lines.

"Yeah, I'm a mustang."

"A tough wild horse?"

Ben laughed. "It's a navy term for a guy who was enlisted and then later became an officer."

"They should teach a course on military language."

"You should be familiar with some of it. Didn't they teach you about the military at Athena Academy?" Ben asked.

"I knew I was going to be a reporter early on. So some of those classes I didn't pay attention in."

"What made you decide to be a reporter?" Tom asked. He tipped his face up toward the sun. Tory wondered if she would be able to survive what he had. Months locked away from human contact, fresh air and sunshine.

"Barbara Walters. I mean, she was the only woman on television when I was growing up and she always got the best interviews. She had a lot of respect in a male-dominated field."

"Makes sense. But why not go into government

work? Athena trains for that, too," Ben said. He tipped his water bottle to his lips and took a long swallow. She watched his Adam's apple bob.

That was what Alex had done. Used her Athena training as a jumping-off point for her career in the FBI. But not all of Tory's friends from those days had chosen the military or government work.

"I don't know. My brother is in the DEA. I needed to be different. I like to be the best at whatever I do."

"I know what you mean. My dad was a marine so I chose the navy," Tom said. When he smiled you could really see the man he was beyond the scars and bandages.

"What about you, Ben? Why are you still in the military?"

"Because there's still a job to be done."

"Patriotism?"

He shrugged and refused to answer.

She knew that was it. Ben Forsythe, scion of the upper crust, was doing a job that few men from any walk of life would risk their lives to do because he believed in freedom and his country. He should have been jaded. Hell, he probably was jaded, but he still did his job.

They continued walking and Tory thought about what her mom had said before she left. About her always having to win.

Tom held his hand up and Ben drew his gun. "Get down."

Tory hadn't heard anything, but she ducked into the thick foliage surrounding the rough path that Ben had cut. Soon the sound of a helicopter filled the air. Tory held her breath, then realized she was being ridiculous. No one would be able to hear her breathing over the noise.

Ben took her elbow and pulled her deeper into the brush. Tom moved in front of Ben and led the way. She ran through the bush, vines scraping against her face and tearing at her clothing until Ben stopped. She slammed into his back. He grabbed her and steadied her.

Then Tom nodded and they moved out again at a run. Tory's lungs were burning, her thighs hurt and she wished she'd left her backpack at the hotel in Paraiso. But she didn't complain. The chopper was quartering the area over them. And she knew that they needed to get as far from the path that Ben had cut to ease their way through the jungle. From the air it probably looked like a big old *X* marking the spot.

Tory kept Ben in her sights and didn't think of anything other than following him. The ground beneath her inclined and she realized they were slowly making their way up one of the foothills of the mountains that lined the interior of the island.

Ben stopped again. Tory tried to control her breathing but couldn't help drawing in deep breaths. "It sounds like they've landed."

Tom lead the way farther into the bush, taking them

up the side of the mountain. There was an outcropping and an opening that was partially concealed by the overgrown vegetation. And Tory, who had always been a sunshine girl, wasn't sure she could go in. But she had no choice.

"Please tell me we aren't going in there."

"What, no story on spelunking in your past?"

"I'll consider this research," she said and followed both men into the darkness.

Chapter 9

The cave was damp and dank. And Tory was reluctant to go inside. "Are there animals in here?"

"Let's hope not," Ben said with one of his half grins. "Stick with Tom. I'm going to do a little recon and cover our tracks."

Fatigue lined his face, but he was alert as he scanned the dense growth behind her. "Okay. Be careful."

"Is that caring?" he asked, running one finger down the side of her face.

"I'm only thinking of Alex and the fact that I don't want to have to drag your body out of here."

"I promise you that won't happen." He used his knuckle under her chin to tip her head back and steal a quick kiss.

Why did he keep doing that? She rubbed her lips as he walked away, reminding herself that they weren't going to be sharing any more kisses and the next time she was alone with Ben Forsythe she was going to set him straight.

She turned toward Tom. "What are we going to do?"

Tom was standing just inside the mouth of the cave, eyes closed and hands clenched. Sweat ran down the side of his face. There was a breeze where they were, so she suspected it wasn't the weather that was making him perspire. She hadn't considered what being back in the dark would do to him.

"Come on. We'll grab Ben and find somewhere else to hide out," Tory said, taking his wrist in her hand.

"No." He refused to budge. Though he was under his fighting weight, he held his ground.

Tory slipped her fingers through his. She led him a little way into the cave. She removed the submachine gun from his shoulders and set it on the floor between them. She did the same with her weapon, but laid it across her lap in case she needed to use it.

She held his hand with hers and started talking. It was what her mom had always done when Tory was little and scared. And one time when Tory had been crying because it seemed her brother and his friends were never scared of anything, her mom had told her that they were just as scared but didn't know how to show it.

"Tell me about your family, Tom. You said you wanted to kiss your wife. What's her name?" she asked.

She'd done little research on the King family. But she wanted to hear about them through Tom's words. And she sensed that Tom needed to talk. To have something other than a closed-off dark space to think about. She knew from their interview how important his family was to him.

"Ellen. She's an attorney." His voice was thin and raspy. Lifeless and flat and it hurt Tory to hear it.

"How'd you meet?" she asked, sitting a little closer to him so he'd know he wasn't alone.

"In Hawaii on leave. I turned around in a bar and spilled my drink down the front of her dress."

"Not the best first impression. How'd you work it out?"

"She's a softy despite being one of the toughest lawyers in Virginia. She can't resist a charming man."

"One in particular, right? Do you have any children?"

"Just a son," he said. "Tyler. He was fourteen when I left. Damn. I've missed so much."

"I'm sorry. I know that's not enough, but I am. Is your son like you?"

"In what way?" Tom asked. His eyes still closed.

"Looks?"

"He's got Ellen's eyes and features but my hair coloring and build. He plays baseball and damned if he's not good at it."

"What do you two do together?" she asked. Tory was prepared to keep the questions coming all night if she had to. But she hoped that Ben returned soon. Tom's grip on her hand was solid and strong—border-line painful.

"Build things. We made a fort in the backyard when he was eight. We made Ellen a gazebo for Christmas."

"I can't build anything. I bought a kit to make a doll-house for my niece and finally I tossed the wood in the fireplace and bought her one that was already assembled."

He was quiet for a minute and she noticed his breathing was starting to even out. His grip on her hand loosened. But Tory didn't let go. Not yet. She wanted to make sure he was okay.

"I'm fine now."

"You always were, Tom."

He opened his eyes. They narrowed as he surveyed the interior of the cave. "We're too close to the entrance."

"I wasn't sure what to do," Tory said, trying not to apologize. She was out of her element and she knew it.

"You did good, girl."

Tom stood and she knew he was operating on sheer guts and force of will at the moment. He led her deeper into the cave, where total darkness surrounded them. "Can we use our glow sticks?"

Tom snapped his on and they found a smooth area of stone where they set up camp. Tom took rations from his pack and Tory ate mechanically. The entire time she kept her eyes on Tom, ready to offer him comfort again if he needed it.

He ate quickly then stood and checked his handgun and slipped the submachine gun back over his shoulders. "I'm going to find Ben and relieve him."

Tory watched him leave and sat there in the dark, wondering if she was going to get off the island alive. There was something dangerous at work against them.

The new government was supposed to be friendly with the United States. Why, then, were they being hunted?

Tory dug her notepad from her backpack and jotted down some things that were bothering her. The glow stick provided adequate light to write. Someone was going to a lot of trouble to stop them from leaving the island. Why?

She had two theories. The first was that American hostages were gold, especially one who was on network television and fairly well-known. She operated under the theory that they didn't know Ben was a Forsythe, but if they did, then that raised the stakes. He had a certain celebrity in the media so he might be recognized. Maybe she shouldn't rule him out.

The second was tied to King's mission. There were too many things that didn't add up there. The ambush for one thing—SEAL missions were extremely secretive. Almost no one knew where the platoons were going until they got there.

She heard a rustling noise at the front of the cave. She picked up the submachine gun and held it loosely in her arms. Then she put the gun down. It was probably Ben or Tom returning.

She had no real skill with that weapon and didn't want to accidentally harm either man. And if the person was a real threat to her, the knife worked better in situations where silence was called for. She took it from the sheath and tried to block the image of the man she'd killed that afternoon.

As soundlessly as possible she made her way toward the noise and felt someone pass right in front of her. She aimed a side kick at the back of his knees and sensed where he fell. But he made no noise. No cursing or anything. It was eerie in the dark.

A hand grabbed her ankle and tugged her off balance. Her assailant controlled her fall, rolling until she was pressed full length underneath him on the cold rock floor of the cave.

She inhaled deeply. The scent of his skin was familiar, and she knew it was Ben.

"Ben Forsythe. It's childish to sneak up on someone."

"Tom said you were in the back of the cave. What are you doing up here?"

"Making sure you weren't a rodent."

He chuckled and got to his feet. He pulled her up beside him. "Lead us back to the area where you and Tom set up camp."

"Is Tom on watch?"

"Yeah. I'll relieve him in a couple of hours."

"No, you won't. I will."

"Tory…"

"What? Don't give me any of that outdated macho crap. I think I proved today that I know what I'm doing."

"It's not macho crap. It's just that you haven't had the kind of specialized training that Tom and I have had."

"I think I can manage."

"We can argue later. I'm hungry."

They came to a stop at the small camp that Tory had set up when Tom had left. Tory snapped on another glow stick and sat down.

She picked up her notepad and settled down on her backpack. The floor of the cave was damp and uncomfortable. Ben took off his khaki shirt and folded it as padding before he sat down.

The T-shirt he wore fit like a second skin, and she forced her gaze away from him as he rummaged around for food and ate. She handed him a water bottle and watched as he took long swallows from it.

"I'd kill for a beer," he said at last.

"Me, too," she said. Anything to give this entire episode some normal tone. This was the kind of adventure that came along once in a lifetime. It was so different from her everyday life.

"Come sit by me. What are you working on?" he asked.

She tilted her head back. "Figuring out why some-one keeps trying to kill us."

"Come to any conclusions?" he asked.

"I've got two theories but I need your help," she said.

Ben roughly shoved his hands through his hair and tipped his head back. His eyes were tightly closed and after a few deep breaths, he turned that electric gaze of his on her.

This mission had probably turned into more than he'd planned on, as well. And she was certain that that brief kiss earlier had been more than just some odd sa-lute to his playboy image. Was Ben affected by her nearness?

"Okay, shoot."

She glanced down at her notes, and suddenly Perry filled her mind. She missed him. He was always a good sounding board and was adept at playing devil's advo-cate and showing her new patterns that she hadn't seen before. She missed the quiet way that he was always there for her.

At the same time, sitting here next to Ben, she real-ized it wasn't Perry whose arms she wanted around her. It wasn't Perry whom she wanted to comfort her.

"First, it's possible that someone recognized you or me and assumes we'd make good hostages. Sec-ond, Shannon Conner, from the ABS network has been following me and trying to steal my story. She may have tipped off the local law enforcement with a bogus story about me being a drug runner. Third, Juan Perez may have decided to get serious about proving he'd changed his mind about letting me interview Tom."

"That first one has merit, at least for you. I took care not to be seen on the island."

"Yeah, right. I saw you three or four times."

"By sticking your nose in where it didn't belong."

"Are you saying the press doesn't have a right to go where the story is?"

"Are you looking for a fight?" He tipped her face toward his.

"Maybe."

"Why?" he asked.

"It distracts me from remembering that guy I killed. And from the fact that we might not make it off the island." She didn't want to feel things. Emotions had always scared her because she couldn't control them.

"The second one is viable, as well. But Shannon Conner really didn't have time to set up a trap. And Perez wasn't in Paraiso last night."

"You're sure?"

"Yes. He left for the U.S. on an afternoon commercial flight, which doesn't mean that he didn't leave orders for you to be kept away from Tom."

He'd given her more information than she'd realized he had. She stared at him, trying to unravel everything in her tired mind.

"What?"

"Nothing." She wasn't going to tell him that she liked the kind intelligence she saw in his eyes.

"Any other theories?" Ben asked.

"Tom's original mission. I might be wrong, but aren't those things usually pretty secretive?"

"You're not wrong. They are highly secretive," he said. He rubbed the bridge of his nose.

She wondered how he was able to keep going. She was tired beyond belief and would kill for a cup of tea and a back rub.

"How could the platoon be ambushed? Am I just buying into propaganda when I believe that our guys are elite and almost unstoppable?" she asked.

"No, it's not just advertising. The SEALs are highly trained and they know how to get in and out with a very high success rate. But someone could have noticed them when they came on the island and set up the ambush then."

"Would the drug runners and Santiago's government have had time to set up their own men as the hostages?" she asked.

He pulled his legs up and leaned his arms on them. He was studying her so intently, it was impossible for her not to be very aware of him. She carefully looked away.

"I'm not sure. What other questions do you have?" he asked.

She pretended she was sitting across from him in the UBC studios doing an in-depth interview. No time for sexual awareness. "Would it be possible for someone to have slipped up and revealed where the platoon was going?"

"Not likely," he said. "That kind of slipup doesn't really happen. But King's mission seems to be the root of whatever's going on here. I wonder what they are trying to hide and who's trying to hide it."

Those were questions she'd like to have asked Perez. But she knew he wasn't going to return any calls from her for a while. She suspected the CIA had been involved in setting up Del Torro's new government. But had they been involved in overthrowing Santiago? And where did King fit into that mess?

Del Torro's government had firmly insisted that all coca-leaf ranchers cease farming and eradicate the plant. She suspected Del Torro was having a hard time enforcing the new policy. It went against centuries of beliefs and practices. She'd seen similar governments go down in flames when the locals fought back against U.S. policy.

"The new government has been playing nice with the U.S., so it doesn't make sense that they'd send their militia after us," Ben said.

"Which leaves the drug runners or coca-leaf ranchers. Do they have choppers?" she asked. She suspected they had planes and probably a good supply of submachine guns like the ones they'd taken from the bandits that had confronted them when they'd left the hotel. But choppers were harder to come by.

"They might. The ranchers are wealthy men. Tom would know better."

"Did you have a chance to speak to Perez or Del Torro?" Tory asked him.

"No. Officially I'm not even on the island."

"What if you die here?"

He shrugged.

"Seriously, Ben. What would Alex and your grandfather be told if you didn't make it back?" Ben and Alex's grandfather Charles Forsythe had once run the CIA. He'd also helped found Athena Academy.

"Nothing. A fatal accident would be staged in Miami. That's where I'm supposed to be."

"Wouldn't you want them to know that you weren't just a playboy?"

He shrugged, but she sensed that he'd made his peace with that type of fate. "What good would it do? I'm not doing this for glory."

She didn't like the thought of his dying somewhere with no one being the wiser. It seemed wrong. "If you die, I'm telling Alex."

He tipped her chin up and gave her a steady look that was steely in its determination. "No, you're not. There's a reason why I'm covert."

"It doesn't seem right. I don't understand—"

He put his fingers over her lips. "I'll explain more later."

She forced her thoughts away from the Forsythe family and back to the problem at hand.

"How long are we staying here?" she asked.

She stuffed her pad and paper away. It was chilly to-night and she rubbed her arms, wrapping them around her waist. She wasn't really good at sitting around and waiting.

"Until the chopper leaves or midnight—whichever comes first," Ben said. He stood and shook out his shirt, tossing it to her. She slid her arms into it. His scent clung to the shirt as did his warmth, and she struggled against closing her eyes and breathing deeply.

"Do you have a plane waiting at the airstrip?" she asked when she saw him gazing at her.

"Yes."

"Let's hope it's in better shape than your vehicle was."

"Let's hope," he said with a grin. He gathered the guns and started checking the safeties and ammunition. Methodically he worked through their small arsenal. When he was finished, he leaned back against the wall and closed his eyes.

"Are you going to sleep?" she asked when she realized he wasn't going to move any more.

"Might as well. Since you don't seem interested in passing the time any other way."

"What a guy thing to say."

"I am a guy."

"I've noticed."

"I've noticed you noticing."

Once they got back to civilization he'd probably not even look twice at her. And she still had a commitment to Perry that she wasn't ready to end. "Did you like it?"

"Yes. You?"

She wasn't sure what he wanted to know. "I haven't noticed you noticing me."

"Well, I do."

"Like it?"

"Hell, yeah," he said. "Come here, Tory."

"No. I'm not even sure I really trust you, Ben."

"What's not to trust?" he asked, standing and walking slowly toward her.

She refused to back away from him. "Everything. You're a chameleon and you change to suit your environment. How can I be sure this isn't just another act?"

"How can I be sure this isn't about your exclusive interview?"

"I guess we can't trust each other," she said slowly.

"You make me crazy."

He tugged her off balance and into his arms. Lowering his head slowly, he gave her plenty of time to back away. But she didn't. She liked the feel of his arms around her. Lifting her hands, she cupped his jaw. Then he kissed her.

It was a slow and deeply carnal kiss that stripped away all the superficial reasons that she'd been storing up in her head to say no to him. She forgot about Perry waiting in New York. And Jay, who'd been flirting with her forever. She was afraid of Ben and what he made her feel because he challenged her.

And he had secrets that she suspected she'd never be able to understand. She lifted her hands, framing his face and trying to take control of the embrace. But he tilted his head to the side and forced hers back.

His tongue made languid sweeps into her mouth, and his fingers on her jaw stroked up and down. His hands slid down underneath his shirt and her T-shirt. He scraped his fingernail along the edge of her bra, and she shivered.

He lifted his head and stared down at her while they both struggled to breathe.

Ben stiffened and pushed her to the side, reaching for his side arm. "What?"

"Shh…someone's coming," Ben said. He lifted his gun and pointed it toward the dark opening of the cave as a figure moved toward them.

Chapter 10

"**P**ut that gun away, stud," said Tom King as he entered the area. Ben flicked on the safety of his gun. Tory shifted farther away from Ben. His hands lingered at her waist, sliding down her leg as she stood up.

"The chopper is in the air again. This time quartering the area with a searchlight. We need to get moving."

Ben nodded and pushed to his feet. His eyes were narrowed in what she was coming to think of as his work mode. "Get your stuff together, Tory."

"I'm ready." Picking up her black backpack by the straps, she waited for her orders.

"Think fast," Ben said.

She glanced up just in time to catch the gear he tossed to her. Night-vision goggles.

Tom gathered his stuff and put on his own NVGs. Ben handed her the submachine gun again. She doubted she'd use it. Tom and Ben had much more skill. But she didn't want to be a liability on this team, and being the only one without a gun could make her that.

Ben handed the second gun to Tom. He slung it over his shoulder. Tory's fingers itched for her camera, but it was too late to really capture what she'd just seen. Two men who had in a moment been transformed into warriors.

As Ben led the way out of the cave into the inky darkness of the night, Tory saw the story unfolding in her head. Scarred and battle-hardened men who fought for their country while most of those they fought for lived their lives unaware.

They spoke little as they walked through the jungle. They made quick time, hiding in the thick brush twice when a searchlight passed over them. For the most part their journey was uneventful.

"This is more like it," Tom said. "There's nothing like night maneuvers."

Ben and Tom talked about the different missions they'd been on. Not in details but in generalities. Talking about the men and the mishaps. The curious part of Tory that always wanted to know what everyone was thinking was in heaven.

She was half a pace behind the men and she listened to their low-voiced conversation. It gave her new insight into Ben. She heard the confidence in his voice when he talked about something that was more than a job to him.

It scared her to realize she was already beginning to care about Ben. Scared her because it could make her weak.

Weak. She let the word bounce around in her mind. Her father had always praised her for being strong. As strong as the boys. At school she'd been praised for being smart and the top in all her classes. At work she'd been praised for her daring. No one ever looked at Tory and saw what she felt every morning.

Weakness and fear that today everyone would see straight through the facade she usually wore and realize she was a fraud. That despite the hard work, she was just skating through life. Carefully keeping from having any personal relationships that were too demanding or too close.

Her closest friends were from her Athena Academy days. Her lover was on assignment away from her more often than not. Her family lived in a different state. And she knew that she liked it that way. That the distance preserved something deep inside her.

Gradually the jungle grew lighter, and finally they were able to remove their goggles. Tom was telling an amusing tale of his first mission when he'd been so eager to be out in the field that he'd stepped out of a vehicle and into a pothole, breaking his ankle. "Some-thing always goes wrong on a mission."

"What went wrong when you came down here?" Tory asked. She'd tried to get Tom to tell her on camera, but he'd refused, saying he hadn't been de-briefed yet.

Tom held back a low-lying branch for Tory. "I don't know. Everything was smooth as silk. We landed early and surrounded the compound. We ra-dioed back to HQ that we were in position and ready to move."

"Then what happened?"

"They asked us to hold."

"Is that odd?"

"Not really. Sometimes satellite footage reveals things that we can't see on the ground."

"So you were in a holding pattern?" Ben asked.

"Yeah. Finally I got the go-ahead and radioed the platoon."

"That's when things went to hell?"

"Yes. The only detail I remember that was unex-pected was a helicopter taking off about fifteen min-utes before we were given the go."

"Did you radio in about it?"

"Yes. They said there were no other choppers in the area. Believe me, I've had the time to think about it and nothing adds up."

Ben brought their group to a halt at the chain-link fence surrounding the airport runways. Tom opened his pack and started digging through it. Ben was doing the same thing.

"I wish I'd more time to talk to the locals. Maybe I'll stay on the island when you guys leave," Tory said.

"No, you will not," Ben said without looking up. He took wire clippers from his bag and began working on the fence. "We aren't sure who is the target of that search."

"My money's on Tom," Tory said.

"You a gambler?" Tom asked.

"Sometimes."

"Then don't put your money on me. Del Torro's government set me free."

"But someone tried to kill you twice in one night. And Ben overheard them talking about taking you back into custody," Tory reminded him.

"We were all in that hotel," Tom said.

Ben stood to continue cutting the fence. Tory stood alongside him.

"Okay."

He nodded. Tom peeled the fence open, and Tory stepped through first. Ben and Tom followed. In a crouching run, they made their way across the open field and hid behind one of the hangars.

"Which plane is ours?" Tory asked.

Ben pulled a small light from his pocket and flashed it twice. An answering flicker came from a small Piper Cub. Tom led the way to the plane, handgun drawn, eyes alert.

Ben followed behind them. Tory felt a new kind of

tension settle over her. The pilot opened the door as they approached the plane.

Before they could climb inside, a bullet sped past them.

Tory flattened herself on the ground and reached for the submachine gun. Ben and Tom were already firing. She glanced at the plane and saw that the pilot was crumpled in the doorway. *Please, let me remember my CPR training.* She'd never taken the time to renew her training. She remembered something about making sure the airway was clear and starting rescue breathing.

She crawled to him and searched for a pulse. She couldn't find one in his neck. She grabbed his wrist. *Please, God, don't let him be dead.* But he was. The shot had hit him in the head. *Dammit.*

Bullets continued to be exchanged around her. She reached up and closed the pilot's eyes. Tory looked at Ben and Tom to see if either of them was going to come over. But they were busy and Tory made her decision. She stood and climbed over the young pilot. Once on board she pulled him back into the plane.

As she leaned over, another bullet came close enough to stir her hair, embedding itself in the metal hull of the aircraft. Tory jumped over the prone man. She tugged him toward the back of the small aircraft and made her way to the cockpit.

Tom and Ben both continued firing in the direction of the assailant, covering each other. Was there more than one gunman or not? Whoever was firing was making judicious use of his bullets. Tory figured the person must be a trained sniper because only the fact that Tom, Tory and Ben weren't presenting clear targets seemed to keep them from being shot.

Tory climbed into the pilot's seat and looked at the instrument panel. She'd taken flying classes at Athena Academy, but it had been years since she'd flown a plane. And then she'd always had an instructor with her.

But she could do this. She glanced around the cockpit and found the button to start the engines. She shrugged out of her backpack so that she'd have more mobility.

Tom came to his feet and fired two more rounds in the direction of their enemy and ran for the plane while Ben covered him. Ben waited until Tom was firing again and retreated to the plane.

Tom went to check on the pilot. Ben jumped in but kept the door open, continuing to fire.

"Take off," he ordered.

Tory steered them out of the hangar toward the runway. The sniper opened fire on the plane and Ben kept firing, holding him back. Tory slowly increased the thrust until the plane started to lift off. The sniper left the cover of the surrounding bush to pursue them.

Ben got off one shot and the sniper went down. The bullet hit the sniper in the chest, and Tory watched as he stumbled and fell. Only then did she notice the long, gold-blond ponytail.

The sniper was a woman. Tory didn't know why she was surprised. But she was. It was always easier for her to believe that the bad guy was a guy.

Tory concentrated on getting the plane in the air. The aircraft banked sharply when they were in the air, and she heard Ben curse.

"Sorry."

She glanced over her shoulder and saw both Tom and Ben lifting the pilot into a seat. Tom took the remaining seat in the back and fastened his seat belt.

Ben joined her in the cockpit. He was dirty and sweating, and there was a scrape on his jaw that was bleeding. He had two days' worth of stubble on his face, and his expression was so fierce that she knew he'd frighten even the strongest of assailants. He was pissed off and still fighting the adrenaline from their near miss.

He holstered his gun and clenched his hands at his sides. "You're one hell of a lady."

She smiled at him. "Thanks. But I can't land this thing. I barely remembered enough to get it off the ground. The pilot's dead, isn't he?"

"Yes." Ben took the co pilot's seat and took the controls. "You did one hell of a job out there."

"Ah, it was nothing. Athena women can do anything."

Tory let go and glanced over her shoulder. Tom had his head back and his eyes closed. There were dark circles under his eyes and a new bandage on his left arm. "Is Tom okay?"

"He took a shot in the arm. The same one that was sprained when we broke him out of the prison." Ben was concentrating on reading the instruments. "Is there a flight plan over there?"

Tory routed around in the papers on the dash until she found the flight plan. Now that they were in the air she set the autopilot. "Want me to navigate?"

He nodded. "Let me look at it for a minute."

She handed it to him and their fingers brushed. She shivered at little at the warmth. She'd come close to losing him. Too close, and it unnerved her.

"Are you okay?" she asked when he looked up at her.

"Fine," he said. She reached for her water bottle and dampened the edge of her T-shirt, then leaned over and wiped the blood off his face.

His breath was warm against her skin.

Ben handed her the flight plan and Tory concentrated on navigating. But inside she was trembling. She wasn't used to being shot at. She wasn't used to adrenaline running through her body. She certainly wasn't used to having people shot and killed in front of her.

"Are *you* okay?" he asked.

"Of course," she said. No way was she going to admit she was seconds away from breaking down. She took one deep breath and then another.

"Your hands are shaking," he said, taking the map from her. He held her hand in his grip. His thumb rubbing over her knuckles.

"I'm not usually a target."

"I know."

"I'll be glad to get back to the real world."

"Me, too."

Twenty-four hours later Tory was in Miami International Airport, waiting for her commercial flight to Manhattan. She hadn't seen Ben or Tom since they'd parted company at the military base a mere four hours ago.

She'd stopped at the local affiliate station and sent her boss, Tyson Bedders, a few clips from the interview so they could start running promo spots. He was saving the opening slot on the evening news for her story. She told him her footage might be rough, but hopefully she'd have time in the edit bay to work on the piece.

Her flight to New York was a direct one and she knew she'd be cutting it close to the wire, but that was okay. This was the kind of excitement she thrived on. Not getting shot at or trekking through the jungle.

It felt so weird to be wearing new clothing and sitting in an air-conditioned airport terminal after all she'd just experienced. She couldn't wait to get home.

Yet at the same time she was a little nervous about the conversation she needed to have with Perry. Though she and Ben probably wouldn't see each other again, she knew it was time to end things with her producer and lover.

She had avoided calling him because she knew he'd

be able to read in her voice that something wasn't right. And she didn't want to have that conversation while he was in one city and she in another. But the past few days had made a few things crystal clear to her, and one of them was that her relationship with Perry was a shield she used.

She hadn't seen or heard anything from Shannon Conner, which was suspicious. Tory hoped nothing had happened to Shannon, but breathed a sigh of relief that the other woman wasn't around.

Tory knew there would be hell to pay if her family found out she'd been in Florida and hadn't contacted any of them. She dialed Derrick's number. Her sister-in-law, Marie, answered. Tory liked Marie. She'd been a grade-school teacher before marrying Tory's DEA brother. Now Marie stayed at home raising their twin boys and younger daughter, all of whom showed every sign of following in their hellion father's footsteps.

"Hey, it's Tory. I'm on a layover at the airport." Tory heard nothing but quiet in the background. Since it was a Monday morning, her nephews and niece were probably at school. The boys, Harry and Joe, were nine, and little Angela was six. They were full of energy and were as curious as Tory ever was. She adored being their aunt and spoiling them.

"How long do you have?" Marie asked. "I can drive down and have a cup of coffee with you."

"I don't have enough time—just an hour."

"Timed it perfectly, huh? Well, Derrick's at work so you won't have to talk to him," Marie said with a laugh.

"Actually I wanted to ask him some questions about the coca-leaf farmers in Puerto Isla."

"I can have him call you when he gets home."

"Good idea. Give those rascal nephews and little angel niece of mine a kiss for me. Bye."

Tory hung up and put her phone away. She pulled the *Times* from her carry-on bag and scanned the headlines. Not too much going on. A few rumblings about the next presidential campaign and a small article about Puerto Isla and how they were trying to entice businesses there.

Good luck. Businesses would take one look at that place and back away fast. Unless something could be done with the drug lords who, as far as Tory had observed, were still a problem there.

She folded up the *Times* and took out the *Miami Herald.* On the society page, she saw Ben's picture. It had been taken at yet another charity event the day before. He again had a lovely blonde on each arm and was grinning at the camera. Tory was a little surprised. Okay, frankly perplexed. How the heck could Ben have been there when he'd definitely been on that plane with her yesterday?

"Hey."

Tory glanced up from under her lashes. Ben Forsythe was leaning against one of the poles in the waiting area.

She wasn't the only one who'd had time to change. Ben had shaved and now wore an Italian silk suit. His hair was perfectly styled, and he had on that sexy but vague grin of his.

Tory raised one eyebrow at him. "What are you doing here?"

"I just finished judging a beauty contest for charity. You know how it is."

"Ah, the life of the playboy. Actually I don't know how it is."

"It's a tough job but someone has to do it."

He sat down next to her and leaned closer. "You look tired."

She didn't smile at him, but she wanted to. "I am. You don't."

"That's because I'm not. I finally had a good night's sleep."

"You did?" She'd tossed and turned, thinking about him and Perry and the sniper. Also, pieces of the puzzle surrounding Tom King were starting to come together. She suspected that the chopper King had reported taking off before their attack was key to what had gone wrong on Puerto Isla.

"Yes, I dreamed of you."

"I think I'm going to be sick. That's the corniest thing I've ever heard."

He leaned back against the seat back and glanced down at the paper in her lap. "Nice photo."

"Not bad."

"How did…?"

"What?"

"Play the innocent all you want. I know—"

He covered her lips with his fingers. "You don't have to say it. I know what you think of my lifestyle."

She nodded. She'd almost blurted out the truth of his whereabouts. "I really am overtired. Not thinking the way I should be."

"I know."

The flight to Manhattan was announced, and Tory wasn't surprised that Ben had the seat next to hers. Once they were seated, Ben lifted the armrest from between them and nudged her head onto his shoulder.

"Don't coddle me, Ben."

"I wouldn't dream of it. But even tough-ass Athena grads need to sleep sometime."

She closed her eyes to tune him out. She warned herself that Ben Forsythe was exactly the type of trouble she didn't need right now. But his shoulder under her cheek was firm and hard. And it comforted her as she finally drifted into sleep.

Chapter 11

Tory's phone rang as she got in the cab at the airport. She glanced at the caller ID and saw that it was the trunk number for her brother at work.

"Hey, Derrick." She'd lost Ben in the cab line and she knew that was probably a good thing. Her life was too complicated right now to have to deal with another man in it.

"Hey, yourself. Marie said you needed to talk to me?" he asked. Derrick was five years older than Tory and had always been very protective and bossy.

"I have a few questions about Puerto Isla and the DEA. There's something fishy with that new government."

"Fishy how?"

"Well, they invited me down there and then refused to let me see my interview subject."

"There have been some pretty steady rumors of some shady deals between the new regime and some U.S. government officials."

"Who?"

"I can't say, but the rumors went pretty high."

"To the U.S. drug czar?" she asked. The U.S. drug czar was the man appointed by the U.S. president to coordinate all aspects of federal drug programs and spending.

"I wasn't able to confirm anything. Keep this close to the chest. The people I spoke to about this were definitely not happy to have questions surface."

"Asking questions is what I do," she said.

"Be careful, Tory. Something doesn't feel right here."

"Derrick, you worry too much." She dismissed his concern. He hadn't wanted her to go undercover inside a women's prison. Yet that story had been the one to bring her to the network's attention.

"You're heading into dangerous waters. Let it drop."

"I'll take your words under consideration," she said.

"And do whatever the hell you want," he said.

"If there is a connection between the drug czar and Del Torro, Puerto Isla's new leader, I can't let the story drop."

"Be careful," he said again and hung up.

Tory leaned back in her seat and realized that each

question she got an answer to generated more questions. The cab stopped in front of the studio and she got out, ready to concentrate on editing the King interview.

Tory rubbed the back of her neck and replaced the phone in the cradle. Her exclusive interview with Tom King was a smashing success. She'd had a few congratulatory calls from colleagues, as well as one from her mother.

"Got a minute?"

She glanced up to see Tyson standing in the doorway. The tall African American man was a dominant force at UBC and in the news world. She liked him as a man, respected him for his integrity and his willingness to go out on a limb for his reporters.

"Sure thing, boss man."

He smiled and entered her office, taking a seat in one of the two guest chairs in front of her desk.

"We were all very impressed with the King interview."

"Thanks. I thought it turned out well. He agreed to a follow-up in a few days' time."

"Do you want to do an uplink this time?"

Tory thought about it for a minute. An uplink would save time, as she'd be able to stay in Manhattan and concentrate on new stories and catch up with the Cassandras on the Athena investigation into Rainy's death and possible child. But she wanted to talk to

King in person. Interview subjects were more open when you sat next to them. "No. There are a few things that aren't adding up. Tom was going to look into them at the base."

"What kinds of things?" Bedders asked. He crossed his legs and leaned forward.

"I'm not sure. I talked to a DEA agent who said there were persistent rumors of money changing hands on Puerto Isla in exchange for DEA and FBI agents looking the other way at certain coca farmers."

"Someone here in the U.S."

"Yes. From what my source told me, the rumors went pretty high."

"How high?"

Tory wondered if she should tell Tyson. He might kill the story before she had a chance to get it off the ground. "Drug czar or higher. My source said that when he asked questions he got shut down in a way that indicated someone very high up knew something they didn't want us to find out."

Tyson leaned back in his chair. "Are you sure you want to go after this?"

"Definitely. Men died, Tyson. Good men who were, if this proves to be true, led to their deaths to cover for a very greedy person."

"Okay. Go to Virginia and follow up with King. Then go to D.C. and shake some cages. I'll get you a temporary office at the D.C. station so you can file stories from there."

"I really appreciate your backing on this, Tyson."

"Make us proud, Tory."

"I intend to."

"Good. Be thinking about what you want for your next contract."

Tory tried not to smile at her boss when he said that. But she couldn't help it. Hard work and perseverance were finally paying off. Her contract would be up for renegotiation in six months' time. "I will."

"Have you considered the weekly newsmagazine offer?"

"I'm still thinking about it. I want to be free to pursue stories like this one. Not trapped behind the anchor desk."

"Bring your wish list to the negotiating table."

Tyson left without saying anything else. Tory leaned back in her chair. Hot damn. Unless she was very mistaken, it sounded as if she was going to be able to write her own ticket at the network.

This called for a celebration. Her first thought was of Ben, but she didn't really have the right to call him. Besides, she was still involved with Perry. She reached for the phone, wanting to share her good news with Perry. At the last second she decided to surprise him.

She called their favorite Italian restaurant, which was just a block from Perry's apartment, and then went downstairs to get a cab. Twenty minutes later she let herself into Perry's apartment with the key he'd given her.

"Perry, I've got good news. And I'm ready to celebrate."

She noticed the wine bottle open on the coffee table and the two half-empty glasses. Setting the food on the counter, she walked farther into the apartment.

"Perry?"

He appeared in the doorway to his bedroom, pants unfastened, hair disheveled and lipstick on his neck. Son of a bitch.

"Is there something you want to tell me?" Tory asked.

Perry rubbed the back of his neck but didn't move toward her. Any guilt she'd harbored about the one kiss she'd shared with Ben evaporated. She swallowed hard against emotions she hadn't thought she'd felt for Perry. Only now, knowing he'd been with another woman, could she face the fact that he'd meant something important to her.

"I wasn't expecting you," he said at last. He ran a hand through his salt-and-pepper hair. He looked every one of his forty-five years at the moment. His lean body showed few signs of age, but his face made up for it.

"Obviously."

Her mother had always drilled into her that a lady didn't embarrass herself or others in awkward situations, but she knew Mom hadn't meant in situations like this.

"Perry?" a familiar feminine voice called from the bedroom. Seconds later, Shannon Conner walked up behind Perry and wrapped one of her arms around his waist.

Betrayal ripped through Tory, weakening her knees. She started toward them and both of them backed up. Tory froze. What did they think she was going to do, kick Shannon's ass? Though in her gut she knew it'd feel good, she wasn't going to. Neither Shannon nor Perry was worth it.

She shook her head and turned to walk out of the apartment. The need to escape was powerful. She stopped thinking and forced her legs to take one step after the other.

Perry grabbed her arm before she got down the hallway. He smelled strongly of sex and another woman's perfume. Not just any other woman's. Shannon's. The one person on the planet who held a grudge against Tory.

"Wait, Tory. I can explain."

Perry's grip on her arm wasn't that strong. Tory shrugged away from him. "I don't care."

"Somehow I knew you'd say that."

She wasn't taking the blame for this. Perry was old enough to keep his pants zipped if he wanted to. This wasn't a spur-of-the-moment lust-beyond-control thing. "You asked me to move in with you, Perry. Do you remember that?"

"And you refused," he said.

"Good thing. It would be crowded in your bed."

He cursed under his breath. "Can we please not do this in the hallway?"

"I really don't care what your neighbors think."

"The network might," he said.

He was right. This was Perry her mentor, not Perry her lover. She knew that as a public persona she had to be untouchable in public. She couldn't even run to the grocery store without getting dressed and putting on makeup. She followed him back into his apartment. Shannon was wearing Perry's shirt and going through Tory's purse.

Tory pushed past Perry and grabbed her purse. Shannon held on to the purse, and Tory brought her left hand down on Shannon's arm with a ridge-hand stroke. Not hard enough to break anything other than Shannon's grip.

Shannon's arm dropped to her side.

"What were you doing, Shannon? Searching my purse for some story that you couldn't find on your own?"

"I don't need to find them with Perry feeding them to me."

Tory turned to Perry. He had his arms crossed over his chest, but in his eyes she saw guilt.

"I'm leaving."

"Shannon, leave us alone for a minute?" Perry asked.

Shannon left the room. Tory stood in the middle

watching Perry. The expression on his face was easy to read. He was sorting through the lies and deciding which ones she might believe.

"How long has this been going on? When did she get back from Puerto Isla?" she asked at last. Because a few things were starting to make sense. Like how Shannon kept showing up at the same place Tory did. Why Shannon kept going after the same stories that Tory was on.

"Since you went to Britain last summer. She returned home from Puerto Isla yesterday. She didn't get a story on the island."

Right before Rainy's death. She stared at him for a moment, unable to believe that he'd betrayed her so thoroughly. Because the Athena piece Shannon had done had been based on a few things that the Cassandras had discovered. "You told Shannon what I discussed with you."

"Like what?"

"The Athena stuff. The stuff about Rainy."

"Maybe."

Liar. He had. She could see it in his eyes. "Maybe? Why? She twisted the facts, Perry. You know that, right?"

"She's not the same kind of reporter you are."

"I know. I won't do a story unless the facts are based in truth."

"I don't want to discuss ethics with you."

"Obviously. Your girlfriend was just going through my purse."

"Ah, hell, Tory. You were drifting away from me. You didn't need me at work or at home. I...I needed a woman who did need me."

All this because she'd wounded his male ego? "You could have said something."

"No, I couldn't have. Nothing gets in your way where your career is concerned."

He was right. "Whatever. I brought dinner, you two enjoy it."

Tory walked out again before he could say anything else. She took the stairs down and hurried past the doorman. The streets weren't busy this time of night, scarcely a car or a person was there. She was alone. She stopped and closed her eyes for a moment, then tipped her head back and looked up at the stars.

My life is screwed up. Rainy, help me. Why can't I stop competing long enough to settle down?

No answers came to her from the stars, and for once talking to her friend didn't help. Perry had been a complication and now he was gone. She could accept the newsmagazine position without worrying about how to bring him along with her. Not that he'd been holding her back, but she'd not wanted to move on without him.

She felt alone despite her many friends and colleagues and her wonderful family in Florida. She didn't have someone else nearby to share the events of her life or to celebrate with, because she'd let almost no one in.

She hailed a cab and gave the driver her address.

Well, at least now she knew where Shannon kept getting all her scoops. That was one less thing to worry about. She'd make sure that Perry was kept out of the loop where her assignments were concerned.

When she pulled her wallet out to pay the cab, a slip of paper fell into her lap. Tory picked it up, thinking it was the receipt from the Italian place.

But it wasn't. "Stop asking questions," the note said.

The handwriting was kind of sloppy. Shannon had slipped over the edge, Tory decided. Especially if she thought this note was going to scare her.

Tory took a long hot shower and climbed into bed. But she couldn't sleep. So she got back out and fixed herself a cup of tea before turning on her computer.

She was a machine, she reminded herself. A journalistic, female machine that got the stories and the answers that no one else could. Slumping forward on her desk, she felt like a broken one.

She'd never done depression well. Her naturally sunny personality always insisted on making her see the bright side.

It had been time to move on from Perry. She wasn't really heartbroken, because she'd never really cared that deeply for him. He'd actually done her a favor.

She just didn't like the way things had ended. She'd had a perfect little speech that she'd planned to give Perry. Something to make him feel better about their parting.

She didn't like losing, and this time she'd definitely not been the winner. But it went deeper than that. How could she have been in a relationship with someone who would betray her so deeply?

Snap out of it.

The words were so forceful she thought that someone had spoken, but no one was in the room with her.

She checked her e-mail and saw one waiting from Lee Chou. She opened the message and skimmed it quickly. He'd found a fertility clinic that had had a break-in around the same time as Rainy's supposed appendectomy.

She skimmed further down the e-mail. The missing and damaged items included donor sperm. One donor whose sperm was listed as unrecovered was…Thomas King. The same Thomas King she'd just helped rescue? Tory began writing on the pad by the computer. She'd ask Tom when she spoke to him.

That was a bizarre connection. And he'd been married at the time, so why would he have donated sperm?

She picked up the phone and calculated the time difference to where Josie lived. It was still a decent hour.

Josie answered on the first ring.

"Hey, it's Tory."

"Hey. I saw your story on the news tonight. Nice job."

"Thanks. The brass liked it, too. I think I'm going to get a big promotion come contract time."

"You deserve it. So why are you calling me?"

"Well...I just heard back from one of my sources at the FBI. There was a break-in at a fertility clinic around the time those surrogate ads that Darcy found ran. And this is the weird part. Thomas King had donated or stored sperm there. His specimen was one of those listed as missing or destroyed."

"Your Thomas King?"

"I'm not sure. But that's an odd coincidence. I'm wondering if I'm missing something here."

"If it is the same man, then we know that he's highly intelligent and skilled."

"That's what I was thinking. Is it a stretch to think this is connected to Rainy? The timing of the burglary is about right."

"I don't know. Have you talked to any of the other Cassandras?"

"Not yet." Tory wasn't sure she could talk to Alex right now. Knowing about Ben's secret life and not being able to share it with her friend would be difficult. "I think I'll put it all in an e-mail and send it to you guys."

"Good idea."

"Josie, I need one more thing."

"Shoot."

"King mentioned that they arrived on Puerto Isla, they were ordered to wait before going in. Do you have access to any surveillance information from that mission?"

"I couldn't share that with you even if I did."

"I just want to know why they were delayed."

"What do you mean, why?"

"I have a DEA source that suggested someone big—
U.S.-drug-czar big—may have been taking a kickback
from the Puerto Isla government."

"So, you think the U.S. government set up King
and his entire platoon?"

"I'm not sure yet. But all of the information I've
gathered points to a connection between the SEAL
ambush and drugs."

"I'll look into it, but I can't promise anything."

"That's all I was hoping for."

Tory disconnected the call. She sipped her tea, letting the information she had stew in her head. She had
a gut feeling that King's sperm had been the target of
the clinic burglary. And that he had no idea his sperm
may have been stolen. But did that have anything to do
with the events on Puerto Isla?

In theory it seemed pretty far-fetched. The fertility
clinic break-in had happened more than twenty years
ago. And the players in this game would have all been
doing different things with their lives.

Her gut said the DEA angle was the key in Puerto
Isla, and she was going to call her brother back in the
morning and pump him one more time for more information.

She did an Internet search to see who the drug czar
had been when the SEAL team was sent to Puerto Isla.
Paul Terrence. Interesting. He'd managed James Whit-

low's campaign for the presidency. She'd call in the morning and see if she could get an appointment with him.

She finished off her tea and leaned back in her chair. Her mind buzzed with possibilities. Some of them were really far-fetched.

One of the first things Tory had learned when it came to unraveling secrets was that you had to start with every plausible scenario.

She wrote down a number one on the yellow pad. Tom King was ambushed because his sperm was illegally used to fertilize Rainy's eggs and the people who did this didn't want him to recognize his kids.

Two. King's sperm had nothing to do with the Puerto Isla events and King and his team saw or heard something that they didn't realize was important.

Three. The person behind the stolen sperm and the DEA connection were the same.

She crossed off number three. That was too strange to contemplate. She rubbed her eyes. She was tired and not thinking straight. But she felt as if the answer was right in front of her.

Chapter 12

Tory's cell phone rang on the way to LaGuardia to catch her flight to Norfolk, Virginia. The cab was making slow progress on this chilly Thursday morning in November. The cabbie was listening to talk radio. "Chris Pearson was in South Dade County this week fund-raising for President Whitlow's reelection campaign next year."

Tory's mind was fixated on Pearson. She'd seen him in Puerto Isla at the presidential palace, just before the start of her troubles.

Tory tuned out the rest of the newscast. It was one week until Thanksgiving. Tory was afraid the caller might be her mother asking if she was coming home for the holiday. She didn't want to leave this story long enough to visit her family for the holiday and she knew her mom would argue about it. But the number wasn't a familiar one.

"Tory."

"It's Marie."

Her sister-in-law sounded tired and upset—as if she'd been crying.

"Where are you calling from?" Tory asked. She had her sister-in-law's cell, home and work numbers programmed into her phone.

"The hospital. Derrick was shot four times last night. Two other members of his team are dead."

"Oh, my God. Is he okay? Do I need to fly down?" What the hell had happened?

"Yes. He's in surgery and should be out soon."

"Are Mom and Dad there yet?"

"They're on their way."

"I'll be there as soon as I can."

Tory disconnected and called her boss, informing him of the situation with her brother. Tyson insisted she go to Miami, saying the follow-up with King could wait. Tory was glad, because if she'd had to choose between work and family, family would win.

She was able to get a stand-by flight that left at almost the same time her flight to D.C. had been scheduled to leave. She rented a car at Miami International and drove quickly to the hospital where Derrick was being treated.

She was directed to the critical-care unit and took the elevator to the proper floor. The first person she saw when she stepped out of the car was her sister-in-law. Tory walked straight to Marie and gave her a hug. Seeing Marie made Tory start crying. The entire flight she'd refused to think about Derrick, her big bear of a brother, being injured.

"How is he?"

"One of the bullets nicked his lung, and it collapsed, but it's reinflated. Dad just went to try to get an update. Your mom took the kids to her house."

"Is he still in surgery?" Tory asked. She wrapped her arm around Marie and moved them to the vinyl-covered seats that lined the wall.

"No, he got out about twenty minutes ago. But we haven't been able to see him."

Marie held tightly to Tory's hand, and though Tory made her living with words, she couldn't find any to comfort Marie. Her own heart was heavy, her mind swirling with a million different scenarios. She refused to settle too long on any of them.

Her dad, William "Buster" Patton, came around the corner a few minutes later. Tory ran to him and he held her close. He was a big bear of a man and his hug engulfed her. She closed her eyes and prayed for his strength. He pulled back and scrutinized her through his dark brown eyes.

"Glad you made it, kiddo."

"What's the news?"

"He's recovering and we can go in to see him in a few minutes."

"Thank God. He's out of the woods?"

Marie went in first to visit with Derrick, then Tory's dad did. Tory stood in the doorway. A wave of helplessness washed over her. Derrick looked vulnerable in that ICU bed, and he'd never looked that way before.

Finally Tory had a chance to talk to her brother. She carefully hugged him and gave him a kiss on the forehead. "How are you?"

"Well, I've been better," he said with some effort, a shadow of the wry grin she was used to seeing on his face.

"I'll say. And you thought my job was dangerous."

"Stop asking questions about Puerto Isla."

"Why?"

"I got an anonymous warning in the locker room before we went out on the raid."

She held his wrist, feeling around until his pulse beat against her finger, reassuring her that her big brother was okay. "Then you got shot. Derrick, I'm sorry. I should never have asked you to poke around in this."

He turned his hand in her grip and held it lightly. "You're not responsible for this. But I don't want to be visiting you in ICU next. So stop."

Could Derrick's accident be her fault? She knew that the person she was searching for had been willing to kill an entire platoon of SEALs. She doubted he'd hesitate to take out a DEA operative. "Don't ask any more questions for me."

"What about you?"

"I'm not letting go of this story. But I'll make sure that I don't contact the family until it's over."

"Just be careful, Tory."

Tory would be doubly careful now. She hugged her brother one last time and left his room. Her dad and Marie were waiting for her. "How long will he be in ICU?"

"We're not sure. The doctor said they might move him to a regular room tomorrow."

"Do you want me to stay and help with the kids?" she asked Marie.

"No, your mom is handling that."

Tory said goodbye to them and drove to her parents' house. She visited with her mother for the afternoon, and booked herself on flight the next morning to Virginia. She called Jay and asked him to meet her in Norfolk. She had a very personal reason to get to the bottom of this story.

The airport was busy with early-morning commuters. Tory let the people flow around her. For the first time the stakes of pursuing a story were raised. Her brother had almost died after asking questions for her. She battled with her own sense of self-preservation for about a second. Before she realized that someone was scared, and scared people always had something to hide.

She hurried to her gate and took a seat in the lounge

area. She opened her laptop and started making notes. She pulled out her yellow pad from two nights ago and looked again at her list of three scenarios.

She needed a second opinion. She needed a different point of view and someone to bounce ideas off of. But she wasn't going to risk any of her friends or family.

She should call Josie and the other Cassandras and warn them to be careful. Although they might take offense. All of them knew how to be discreet. That was another thing that Rainy and Athena Academy had taught them. Her heart lurched, and for a minute she allowed the anger that had lingered at Rainy's untimely death to flood her.

She needed her friend's advice. But Rainy was gone. Tory was on her own despite having five Athena friends. She didn't want to risk anyone else getting hurt because of a story she was pursuing.

On her own.

Her heartbeat sped up and that weird elixir of fear, excitement and anticipation buzzed in her veins. She shivered and closed her eyes, visualizing the end result. Visualizing her story coming together.

"Miss Patton?"

Tory glanced up. A young man with one earring in his left ear and a tattoo on his neck stood there. His hair was spiked and his eyes lined with thick black eyeliner.

"Yes?"

"Here," he said, thrusting a piece of paper at her. He walked out of the lounge.

Tory opened the note and immediately saw the American-eagle insignia that was AA.gov's trademark. The note was brief and asked her to go the rest room to receive a package to deliver to the naval air station in Norfolk.

Tory tucked the note into the pocket of her blazer. Though she hadn't sent a note to the courier group to tell them her plans, she wasn't surprised to be contacted. The group was highly connected.

Tory put away her laptop and notes and left the lounge. The bathroom facility wasn't busy when she entered, and she glanced around for her contact. A woman in a dark blue suit came up next to Tory at the mirror.

Tory pulled her bright red tube of lipstick out of her purse. The woman next to her had an identical tube. Tory set her purse on the counter and leaned closer to the mirror. She saw the woman's hand flash briefly and deep into Tory's purse. A moment later, the woman turned and left.

Tory saw the small brown envelope sitting on top of her wallet. She dropped the lipstick into her purse and zipped it shut before leaving the bathroom.

A short while later, Tory was on the plane on her way to Thomas King and, hopefully, the answers to some of the more bizarre questions surrounding this story.

Jay was waiting for her at the rental-car counter at the airport in Norfolk. He'd come from D.C., where he'd been covering the latest Washington tug-of-war. President James Whitlow's recommendation for the empty Supreme Court seat was being met with a lot of opposition.

But then, most of Whitlow's presidency had been filled with strife. Even his campaign had fallen under intense public scrutiny. Tory had covered some of the fall-out from that. He'd had a lot of contributions to his campaign from the business sector.

"I was beginning to think I should go ahead without you."

"Funny, Jay. You might be a talented cameraman, but you don't know the questions to ask."

"I'm sure I could wing it."

"It takes talent and experience to do a good interview."

He gave her a cheeky grin. "Then why are yours always well received?"

She punched his arm and took the keys from him. "Wise-ass."

They made their way to the rental, a truck with four-wheel drive. "Can you handle this truck?"

"Hell, yes. I grew up on a ranch in Florida. I learned to drive on a truck."

"Is there anything you don't know how to do?" he asked.

There were a few things. But she was careful to never let anyone notice them. She was of the school of never let anyone see you sweat. "I'll let you know when I find out."

Tory noticed a couple of other reporters from rival networks at the airport. She knew Thomas King was on everyone's radar. But Shannon, thank God, wasn't there. Tory still felt a simmering anger toward the other woman. Shannon had a vendetta against her. First going after Perry, then Athena.

Tory forced thoughts of Shannon to the back of her mind but she was still angry and would like nothing better than to expose Shannon for the hack she was. But that would have to wait.

It was dusk by the time they headed toward the King household. Tory called her parents while they were driving and learned her brother was doing well.

Tory parked in the Kings' driveway and she and Tory got out of the truck. It was cold out, and she tugged on her leather gloves. She reviewed her notes. "Ready?"

Jay nodded and they approached the brick house with its neatly landscaped yard. A basketball hoop hung over the driveway of the three-car garage, and a ball rested in the shrubs. Two bikes stood by the front yard.

Tom opened the door for them. He looked one hundred percent healthier than the last time Tory had seen him. He'd asked to keep his reunion with his wife private, but had agreed to give UBC and Tory this interview on the Kings' home turf.

"Hello, Tom. Are you enjoying being back in the States?"

He nodded and stepped back. Tonight he looked like any other guy in suburban America. He wore a pair of chinos and a plain black sweater. Most of his visible wounds had healed. "Come in."

"Do you remember Jay? He's going to be shooting us again."

The men shook hands. The hallway of the King home was adorned with navy plaques and pictures of the small family of three at different holidays. "We'll let Jay mike you."

Tory glanced up to see a very attractive woman coming down the stairs. She was tall, at least five-seven, and curvy. She had a warm smile and thick blond hair that fell in waves to her shoulders. "This is my wife, Ellen."

Tory stepped forward and shook Ellen's hand. "It's nice to meet you. Thank you for letting us come to your home. Where can we set up for the interview?"

Ellen led the way to a formal living room. It reminded Tory of the room in her parents' house where no one was allowed to wear their shoes, drink coffee or eat. While Jay set up the equipment and miked Ellen, Tory turned to Tom. "Can I speak to you alone?"

"Sure," Tom said. They stepped back into the foyer. He crossed his arms over his chest and leaned against the door frame.

Tory took a deep breath. She'd asked some tough questions in her years as a reporter and she didn't want to just blurt this one out. "I have an odd question for you. Did you ever visit a fertility clinic?"

He seemed surprised. He ran his hand through his thick blond hair. Then he took her arm and led her away from the opening leading to the living room. "As a matter of fact, yes. That was back when Ellen and I were newly married, before we had Tyler. Because of the nature of my job, there was always a possibility that I might not make it back or would come back in bad shape. And Ellen and I wanted kids."

"I understand." Her brother had done the same thing before Marie had given birth to the boys. Then they'd asked to have the sperm destroyed. Men who laid their lives on the line every day had to consider things that most didn't. "Are you familiar with the Athena Academy?"

"Yes. I didn't mention it when we were on the island, but I taught a course there for a semester."

"How long ago?"

"It was during the first year that the school actually opened. Why do you ask?"

"I've been researching some odd things pertaining to Rainy Miller. Lorraine. She would have been Rainy Carrington when you were there."

"I remember her. She was one of my strongest students."

"Rainy was recently killed," Tory said. Tears burned the back of her eyes. Suddenly she felt the loss more powerfully than she had since she'd first gotten the call. She wrapped her arms around her waist and took a deep breath.

"Bear with me, because this is going to sound a little strange. An autopsy was performed, and it revealed some scarring on Rainy's ovaries. We believe her eggs were mined, way back when she was an Athena student. In the process of our investigation, we found out that your sperm had been stored at a fertility clinic in Arizona that was burgled around the same time."

"Who is 'we'?"

"My group of friends from Athena. Rainy was our group leader for our first year at Athena."

"What does this have to do with my sperm? We were contacted about the break-in. The authorities were certain that sperm wasn't the object of the break-in. Samples were destroyed randomly as the burglars went through the office."

"We don't know. But we are continuing to look into it. What were you teaching at Athena?"

"Special-ops techniques."

"When I was at Athena we had a Green Beret." Athena had close ties to the military and each year they rotated in different experts from all the military branches.

"Is everything okay, Tom?" Ellen called from the living room.

She and Tom went back into the living room to get ready for the interview. Tory put aside the information Tom had given her. She couldn't wait to let everyone know what she'd found out. But the new information only led to more questions.

* * *

Ellen and Tom sat on a brocade-covered love seat. On the end table next to them were their wedding picture and a picture of Tom and Tyler, their son. Tory took a deep breath and started asking questions.

"Tom, what was the first thing you did when you got home?" she asked. The camera was trained on Tom and Ellen, so Tory didn't have to worry about how she appeared. She kept her notepad in her hand so she could take notes, as well.

Tom put his arm around his wife. "Hugged my wife and son."

"How has life changed for you since you've been back?" Tory asked. She could see that the couple was happy to be back together. "Ellen, how does it feel to have your husband come back from the dead?"

"Wonderful and unreal sometimes. I don't want to let him out of my sight for a second because...I'm afraid I may have dreamed that he's alive."

Tom put his arm around her shoulder and hugged her close to his chest, whispering something in his wife's ear. She smiled up at him and then shifted back to her own seat. Tory noticed the Kings still held hands.

"What's life like now, Tom?"

"I'm still adjusting to being out of prison and having a normal routine again."

"Will you be going back on active duty?"

Tom glanced at Ellen, then back at Tory. "As soon as I'm cleared by my doctor."

"Ellen, how do you feel about that?" Tory asked. From her body language Tory knew that Ellen wasn't too happy to have her husband risking his life again.

"I'm very proud of my husband and his service to his country."

"We all are. But isn't there a part of you that wishes he'd stay home?"

"There's always a part of me that worries for him and for the risks he takes. But he wouldn't be the man I love if he didn't take them." She tipped her head toward Tom. He squeezed her closer to him with his arm, and for a minute Tory felt a pang of longing.

Tory was reminded of Ben. And she knew that deep inside in the vulnerable place that she didn't want to acknowledge she had, she felt the same way.

"I think we can all understand that. Tom, we didn't really have a chance to discuss your captivity in our first interview. Would you mind telling me a little about that time?" She'd asked him about it when they'd been trying to get out of Puerto Isla, but not on camera.

"What do you want to know?" Tom asked. He lifted his arm away from Ellen and sat up straighter.

"Were you questioned?"

"I was questioned repeatedly about what I saw on the island."

His eyes were hard as glass, and all of the love and affection he'd displayed just moments earlier toward his wife were carefully concealed now. She realized she was glimpsing the warrior she'd met on the island. "And how did they react to your answers?"

"They didn't believe anything I said. Each day they asked the same questions again and again."

"What questions did they ask?"

"What was I doing there? When did I arrive on the island? Where had I gone? How had I found the camp? Those types of questions."

She sensed he was ready to end this line of questioning. Especially in front of Ellen. She resolved to finish the interview as quickly as possible. "Who held you captive?"

"The Puerto Isla government, under Diego Santiago."

"Once he was kicked out of power by Alejandro Del Torro's rebel group, were you freed?"

"No. I didn't know of the change in government until I was rescued."

"By who?"

"Another SEAL team."

"How?"

"I can't really say much, but they were able to get me off the island."

"Ellen, how did you feel when you first learned your husband had come back from the dead?" Tory asked.

Ellen reached for her husband's hand and held it in both of hers. "I cried. At first I didn't believe it."

"When did you finally accept your husband was alive?"

She never took her eyes off of Tory, but Tory noted that Ellen's hands tightened around her husband's. "When I held him in my arms."

"Thank you both for speaking to me."

"You're welcome, Tory."

Tory nodded and then turned to face the camera. The interview was concluded and would run tomorrow night as part of UBC's weekly newsmagazine, but she needed to wrap up from here. "The Kings will be in Washington, D.C., later this month for a celebratory dinner honoring United States Navy Commander Thomas King. I'm Tory Patton, UBC News, reporting from Little Creek, Virginia."

They turned off the mikes and Tory turned back to the couple. "Do you mind if Jay shoots some cutaways of your house?"

"No. Not at all. I'll show him around," Ellen said.

Jay and Ellen left the room. Tory took off her mike and put her notepad back in her purse. She wanted Tom to relax. She needed some answers from him. Answers to questions she didn't intend to ask on air. At least not yet.

"Tom, is it possible that your platoon was set up?"

He shrugged and leaned back against the couch. "How?"

"I have a source in the DEA that I asked about the Puerto Isla situation, and he suggested that perhaps someone from the U.S. government was on the island when you were there."

"It's possible. As you know, the DEA and FBI are very active in Central America, working to ensure the eradication of the coca leaf."

"But they aren't always successful." Tory knew this from the struggles the U.S. was encountering in many South and Central American nations, including Bolivia.

"No, they aren't. I'm really not sure."

"Did you see anything on the satellite photos while you were ordered to wait?" she asked.

"Our satellite equipment blinked out, and we had to wait to put it back to move."

"I have a theory. Will you tell me if it makes sense to you?"

"Sure."

"Let's say that someone from our government was down there meeting secretly with the drug lords and didn't know your team was coming in."

"It could be possible, but our orders come from pretty high up. So this shadow government man would have to have been connected but not with the military. And then when we reported that we were moving in, someone would have had to realize we were there."

"Could that have happened?"

"It's possible, but why?"

"I'm not sure. Who is the American ambassador to

Puerto Isla? He'd know which government officials were present when your team went in."

"It's David Addler."

"Did the prison guards ask you about him and his office?"

"No. Addler, his team and all U.S. personnel were evacuated from Puerto Isla after my team was killed."

"I'm going to contact Addler."

"Good luck, Tory. And if you find out anything about the other matter, the clinic break-in, will you keep me advised?"

"Yes. I'm going to pass your number on to the other Cassandras. There are six of us. Josie Lockworth, Darcy Steele, Alex Forsythe—she doesn't know that her brother, Ben, is anything but a playboy by the way—Samantha St. John and Kayla Ryan."

"Copy me on the e-mail so I can have their contact information."

"I will. And if you think of anything else about Puerto Isla, please let me know."

Jay shot Ellen, Tom and their son, Tyler, sitting at the kitchen table drinking soda and coffee. He also got Tom and Tyler playing video games and Ellen watching them both. Then he shot Tory asking her questions with the camera on her.

Satisfied with all the shots they'd gotten, they packed up to leave. Jay got everything in the rental truck while Tory said goodbye to Tom. She was halfway to the rental vehicle when something whizzed by her head, stirring her chin-length hair.

She dropped to the ground as she realized that it was a bullet and someone was firing at her.

Chapter 13

Tory tucked her body and rolled into the covering brush. Branches caught at her wool coat, and she lost her cashmere scarf. Scanning the area to the west of the house, she tried to find the sniper. But she couldn't see anything. It was too dark.

Lying as still as possible, she waited about a minute before deciding to chance moving toward the vehicle. Where was Jay? Had he been hit?

She crawled on her belly toward the car, staying in the shadows. She heard the distant sound of an engine starting.

She jumped to her feet and ran to the rental. Jay already had the truck running. She slid into the passenger seat.

"Jesus. Was it my imagination or was someone shooting at us?" Jay said.

"We were definitely being shot at." Tory took her cell phone from her bag and dialed King's number. He answered on the first ring.

"Someone just shot at Jay and I as we left your house."

"Are you in danger?"

"We're both in the truck and I just heard an engine start. I believe our assailant got away. Should I call the police?"

"Let me take care of that. Be careful, Tory."

She rang off with Tom. And turned to Jay. He'd reached over the seat and pulled a flask out of his camera bag. He took a deep swig and then offered her the flask.

"No, thanks. Did you hear that engine start? Let's see if we can find them."

Jay drove west, in the direction that Tory indicated she'd heard the car start. "The shooter was using a silencer."

Jay nodded. He gripped the steering wheel firmly with both hands. She wondered if he had the shakes as she did. She was sick and tired of being shot at. It was unnerving to think someone was out there looking for them. The shots were too well placed for Tory to doubt that someone was warning them. But who?

"A bullet nicked the back of the truck when I was stowing the equipment."

"Are you okay?" she asked.

"Yeah. Pissed, but otherwise fine."

They caught a brief glance of some taillights before the car turned onto the divided highway and blended with the traffic. Tory's pulse was racing and her heart hammered inside her head.

"This is getting to be routine," Tory said. She was ticked off and more than a little worried. The stakes were higher than she'd believed possible. She might have stopped digging if someone hadn't kept trying to kill her, but now she wouldn't.

"What is?" Jay asked.

"Getting shot at." She wondered if Ben ever got used to it. And if he did, what tips could he offer her.

"I had no idea that journalism was so dangerous."

Tory knew it could be. There were many times when she'd heard of reporters being pulled off cases or, when they refused to give up, killed. "I think Veronica Guerin proved that point."

"She did. But you're not investigating a drug ring."

"I think I am, Jay." Tory rubbed the back of her neck. The note in her purse might not have been from Shannon. It could have been from the AA.gov woman. In fact, Tory remembered bumping into someone at the airport. Maybe someone had been warning her since she'd been back in the States. "This is the second warning I've had in as many days."

"What was the first one?" he asked, glancing from the road at her. His features were craggy in the low light from the dashboard.

She didn't want to give Jay too much information. Her gut said that danger was lurking and she didn't want to be responsible for anything happening to Jay. "There was a note in my purse that said to stop my investigation."

"So you've seen this person?"

"Maybe. I didn't realize I'd received a warning. And it could have happened at any time."

"Why do you think the shots were a warning?" Jay asked.

"Because we're both still alive. That shooter didn't miss by mistake."

"How can you be sure?" he asked.

"I can't be, Jay. But my gut tells me I'm right."

"Should we file a police report?"

"Tom said he'd take care of that."

"Where to, boss lady?"

"The airport. I want to get this story back to New York and edit it. Them I'm going to D.C."

"Do you need a cameraman?" he asked as he maneuvered the truck from the small country highway onto the interstate heading toward the airport.

"I think I'd better go alone. I'll take the camera purse with me."

Tory sank back into the seat while Jay drove quietly back to the airport. She still had her courier package to deliver. Dammit, she'd forgotten about that.

"Jay, pull into that convenience store up ahead."

"We don't need gas."

"I need to stop."

Jay pulled to a stop and Tory got out. She hurried into the store and the rest-room facility, which was one of those big one-person rooms. She called AA.gov.

"This is Tory Patton. I need to speak to Agent M."

"One moment, Patton."

She held the line. In the mirror over the bathroom sink she saw her own reflection. She looked tired and rumpled. She detected a faint trace of fear in her eyes and stared hard at herself until the fear was replaced by determination. She brushed the leaves and twigs off her clothing.

"This is Agent M."

"I'm not going to be able to make my drop in Norfolk."

"We don't have you down to deliver anything."

"I picked up a package at LaGuardia this morning."

"What's in it?"

Tory pulled the brown envelope from her purse and opened it.

First your brother, then you. Stop now before someone dies.

Shuddering, Tory almost dropped her phone. "A note. It's for me."

"What does it say?"

Tory shook her head. "Nothing important. A warning pertaining to the story I'm working on. Don't use me as a courier for a while."

"Why not?"

"I think I've been compromised. And I think the organization has been, too. They knew our signals and codes. The drop was conducted in the bathroom and my orders were on AA.gov stationary."

"Did you destroy the first contact note?"

"Yes."

"I need you to bring the note you still have to our offices in D.C."

"Yes, ma'am."

Tory left the bathroom more determined to get her story than ever. She knew that she couldn't take the chance of involving anyone else in her investigation. The more clues she got, the more complicated and dangerous this story became.

Tory arrived in D.C. on Monday morning. She'd filed her follow-up story on Thomas King. She'd also let the Cassandras know that King had taught at Athena. The connection was almost coincidental, but Tory had a feeling that there was more there than she was seeing.

She was tired and cold. So damned cold. Growing up in Florida didn't acclimatize one to November in the Northeast. She ordered a pot of tea from room service just before lunchtime and went over her notes.

One of the secretaries at the network had worked all day to get Tory an appointment with David Addler, former U.S. ambassador to Puerto Isla. She was scheduled to talk to him at four o'clock this afternoon.

Addler had gone into semiretirement since he'd left Puerto Isla. His term had ended just after King's platoon had been killed. Since that time Addler had been working as a freelance consultant for ABS, Shannon Conner's network, giving some perspective on political situations in Central America.

Tory jotted down a few questions for Addler. She really wanted to talk to Paul Terrence, the U.S. drug czar, but so far his office had refused to make an appointment for her. Now that she was in D.C., she had no problem camping out at his home or office until he caved in.

Someone knocked on the door and Tory went to answer it, expecting her tea from room service. But when she checked through the peephole, she saw Ben Forsythe standing there.

She opened the door and stepped back. He entered the room and quickly closed the door behind him.

"Hello, Ben."

"Tory, what the hell is going on?"

She calmed her rapid heartbeat. She hadn't been thinking about Ben and lust and the screwed-up mess her personal life was until he'd barged right back into it. "I'm not sure. What are you talking about?"

He gave her a look that she was sure sent young recruits scurrying to do his bidding. "You getting shot at in Virginia."

"How do you know about that?" She'd talked to Tom twice since then, as well as to the local police. She and Jay had taken the rental vehicle to the police station. So far they had no leads on whoever had shot at them. To be on the safe side, Tom had taken his family on a vacation to Hawaii.

"I know everything."

"Everything?" she asked with a slight grin. "Bennington Forsythe, playboy, secret agent and now…possessor of the second sight."

"Don't try to change the subject. I don't want you taking chances with your life."

Why? She wanted to know but wasn't going to ask. She didn't need the kind of complications this man could bring to her life. She liked everyone to fit in the nice, neat little corners she assigned them. Her family and the Cassandras fell into an emotional place, her job and courier work into an exciting place. Men always fell into the "nice to have around for a while but not the long haul" place.

"I'm not. I'm following a story. If there's a risk involved I'm willing to chance it."

"I'm not."

"Ben…don't do this. We agreed—"

"Bullshit. I didn't agree to anything. And dammit, I'm not asking for anything other than a little caution from you."

"I'd be happy to comply, but I have no idea what to be cautious about. I'm still connecting the dots."

He ran his fingers through his hair, watching her with that enigmatic blue gaze of his. No one had ever rushed to her side when she'd been in trouble before. Her dad had always told her to shake it off, her friends all knew she'd pull through and yet here was Ben. She knew she shouldn't be, but all the same she was touched that he'd come to D.C.

"Tell me what you have so far."

He didn't ask; he just naturally took command. But this was her story and she wasn't surrendering her information easily. Derrick's injuries were related to the questions he'd asked for her. She didn't mind risking herself. But putting Ben at risk…she wasn't prepared to do that.

"I'm not sure I should tell you."

"I have a high security clearance. If the government trusts me, can't you?"

"That's a corny line and I think you got it from *Top Gun*."

"I know it's one of your favorite movies. And if it worked for Cruise it should work for me."

"How do you know I like that movie?"

"Alex mentioned it the last time we were at our grandfather's house. It was on TV late at night, and we were hunkered down in the den eating salty popcorn."

"With *your* grandfather?"

"Don't let the old man's image fool you. Underneath that retired-CIA-director facade, he's still just a grandfather."

She knew that Charles Forsythe was responsible for how both Alex and Ben turned out. She wondered if the shrewd old man realized that Ben was more than a globe-trotting playboy. Probably.

She pulled back and leaned against the dresser, crossing her arms over her chest. Ben stared at her, one eyebrow arched in question. She had the feeling he'd wait all day if that was what it took.

Finally she sighed. She didn't like being reminded that Ben had a close-knit family. She shouldn't have allowed him to become involved in this story. "I don't want to put you at risk."

"I've got news for you, Tory. If you're at risk, I'm not leaving you alone."

She wasn't ready to have a man in her face like this. Ben disturbed her on many different levels, and the scary part was that sometimes, deep in the night when she was all alone, she liked it.

"One of my sources was shot after asking some questions for me."

"Your brother, Derrick, right?"

"How did you…?" She trailed off. He did know everything. "Yes, my brother. I don't want you in danger, either."

"I'll consider myself warned."

She didn't want him just warned. She wanted him safe. And Ben wasn't the kind of man she could tell to stay put. He'd been trained probably since childhood to right wrongs and seek justice. "Ben…"

"Tory…"

"You are so damned stubborn."

"Yeah, it's one of my more appealing qualities."

"Keep telling yourself that."

"I will. In the meantime, what's going on with this story?"

She crossed the room to the padded armchair. "King's team definitely witnessed something or saw someone they shouldn't have. I have a friend trying to get the satellite surveillance photos from that night. From what Tom remembered, I think the hostages were already dead before the team got there."

"It fits what I've been told."

"What else do you know?"

"I'll tell you when you're done."

"I've spent the afternoon on the phone and on the Internet, tracking down information. So far, I know that Ambassador Dave Addler was still on the island along with another high-ranking official—I've haven't found out who yet. I also know that Addler retired really quickly after the SEAL incident."

"Have you spoken to Addler?"

"Not yet. I'm going to see him later today. He might be able to tell me more about the hostage situation."

"I can fill you in on some details there. The hostages were part of Doctors without Borders. Three men, one woman. They'd been on the island for about nine months when they were captured by a group of anti-American drug runners and coca ranchers."

"Did they demand anything for the hostages?"

"Yes. That the U.S. continue to provide financial aid

to the government and back down on its total eradication of the coca-leaf policy."

She processed that. "Why kill the SEAL team, then?"

"I don't have that information. I asked a few questions when we got back and was told to forget about it and move on."

"Then what are you doing here?"

"I've been asking myself that very same thing."

Tory and Ben had split up when they left her hotel room. He'd offered to let her stay at his apartment in Crystal City, Virginia. Tory wanted to so badly but in the end she'd said no. Ben distracted her and she needed to think clearly to pull this story together. Besides, she didn't want to risk the two of them being seen in public together.

She took the Metro Redline to Georgetown and walked the few blocks from the station to Addler's residence. The sun was shining this afternoon, and though the high was only fifty degrees, Tory was comfortable in her overcoat. She adjusted the purse camera, pausing to turn it on outside the former ambassador's residence.

The housekeeper answered the door and directed her down a short hallway to Addler's den. Addler was in his sixties but fit and trim. His hair was gray but not thinning. He held a cigar loosely in one hand. He stood when she entered the room.

He wore a pair of khaki chinos and a button-down Oxford shirt with the cuffs rolled back. She noticed he had a black tattoo on his forearm. She wondered if he'd gotten it in Vietnam. Her dad had one from back then.

"Good afternoon, Mr. Addler. Thanks for taking the time to see me."

"No problem, Ms. Patton. Please call me Dave."

"And I'm Tory."

Addler resumed his seat and gestured for Tory to sit in one of the leather armchairs. "Can I offer you something to drink?"

"I'm fine."

"What do you want to know?"

"I'm trying to do some background on a more in-depth story I'm working on about Puerto Isla. I had a chance to talk to several locals while I was on the island and I'd like to get a different perspective of what was going on when Tom King and his team went in to rescue the Doctors without Borders hostages."

"Well, it was very chaotic. I've heard the island is a lot better now that Del Torro is in charge. Fighting between the government and the people was erratic. Santiago kept most of them under control with his militia. But then Juan Perez and Del Torro banded together. Once they started getting organized, it was the beginning of the end for Santiago."

"But Del Torro's government has even stronger ties with our country than the old government, isn't that right?"

"Yes." He leaned back in his chair and took a drag on his cigar. He pivoted in his chair and looked out the window.

Tory had a feeling that he was looking at Puerto Isla in his mind. "Why is that?"

He glanced over his shoulder at her and then spun back to face her. He set his cigar in a crystal ashtray and leaned forward, elbows resting on the top of his mahogany desk. "I can't really say. I'm no longer the ambassador there."

"No, you're not. But you are very familiar with Central America." Tory wasn't sure what to ask to get him to open up. What she really wanted to know was if Paul Terrence had ever visited the country. But she didn't want to ask such a blatant question.

"I can only say that someone wants us to believe that things have changed on Puerto Isla."

"Haven't they?" she asked.

Addler shrugged. "Was that all you wanted to know?"

"No. Who called in the SEALs?"

"I did."

"Would you walk me through the taking of the hostages, and your office's involvement?"

"We were notified of the hostages almost immediately. We verified they'd been taken and I asked for military assistance in retrieving them."

"Who from the military did you talk to?"

"General McKinley."

"What happened then?"

"I was put in contact with King. I gave him the co-ordinates and I didn't hear anything more about the team until I learned they'd all been killed."

"Did you know King had been taken prisoner?"

"No. I believed they had all been killed."

Tory jotted a few notes on her notepad. Though she was recording the interview on her secret camera, she wanted a written account of the interview, as well.

"How long were you in Puerto Isla?"

"For two years."

"During that time were there any other incidents like this one?"

"Only one. It took place when I first arrived on the island."

"American hostages?"

"Yes. But they were rescued."

"Who were they?"

"I'm not at liberty to say."

Interesting. "Did you have any visits from American officials while you were there?"

"Of course."

"I know the coca-leaf topic was a hot one—was anyone ever sent down to discuss it with the government?"

"No. After the SEAL incident and the killing of the hostages, the U.S. pulled completely out until the new government was put in place."

"Would you be willing to do an interview with me

on air?" she asked. She knew it was a long shot. She wasn't even sure Tyson would let her speak to him on air without prior approval. As far as protocol went, she was supposed to talk to Tyson or one of the producers before she scheduled an on-air interview. But she thought it was better to ask.

"I think my contract with ABS precludes that. I'm already scheduled to do one with Shannon Conner."

She smiled. She definitely wasn't doing any interviews that could be compared with Shannon's. Tory planned to move beyond her rival in such a way that the two women would never be mentioned together again. "Thank you for speaking with me."

"Not at all. I hope I helped."

Not really, she thought. But then, he knew he hadn't given her any answers. Was he hiding something? Her gut said he was. But she'd have to go away and come at this from a different angle.

Chapter 14

Tory returned to her hotel room in the Capitol district. She had a million things running through her head. She needed a break. She knew she was missing something vital and elemental to dissipating the cloud that hung over this story. Everyone she'd talked to had another piece of the puzzle and no matter how she twisted and turned them they wouldn't fit together.

What was the crux of the matter? Drugs definitely played a part, and a government official—possibly Paul Terrence or Dave Addler. And then there was the Puerto Isla government, and their odd tap dance involving the SEAL platoon and then the freedom of Thomas King.

She typed up her notes and reviewed the interview

with Addler. He was an interesting man. Her instincts said he wasn't telling her the full truth. She did an Internet search on him and found out he'd spent his entire career in South and Central America.

Tory recalled an interview she'd seen when the Addlers had returned to the States. Perry had produced the piece for veteran newscaster Cal Jones. He had to know more than he was willing to tell her. David Addler's wife, Charlotte, had not liked living in Puerto Isla.

Mrs. Addler was a beautiful woman but she'd been worn down by her time on the island. Tory replayed the interview in her head. She'd been in the editing room when Perry had put the piece together. They'd had a hard time finding shots of Mrs. Addler that worked. Her interview had been lackluster.

Tory grabbed the phone and placed a call to the Addler residence.

"May I speak to Charlotte Addler, please?"

"Who is calling?"

"Perry Jacobs's office from UBC. We're doing a follow-up to our previous interview." She'd just been in the house, so she didn't want the housekeeper to realize who she was.

"Hold, please."

Tory waited.

"I'm sorry, Mrs. Addler is traveling. May I take a message?"

"When do you expect her return?"

"I'd be happy to relay a message to her."

"With whom am I speaking?"

"The housekeeper, Mrs. Tolleron."

"Did you work for the Addlers when they were on Puerto Isla?"

"No. Is that all?"

"Yes." Tory disconnected the call. It wasn't the lead she'd hoped for.

Tory rubbed the back of her neck. She was getting nowhere. She stood up and stretched. Then she fell backward onto the bed. Staring at the ceiling, she tried to quiet all the questions spinning around in her mind but she couldn't.

She reached for the camera purse and pulled the small unit toward her. Rolling over onto her stomach, she sprawled on the king-size bed in the middle of her suite and sorted her notes into piles. She watched the tape of Addler one more time and spotted a picture on the wall over his desk that she hadn't noticed when she'd been in his den.

It was a photo of Dave and Chris Pearson. Tory froze the frame and squinted at the small screen. They were on a boat in a marina. The coastline looked familiar to Tory. She'd been to that marina with her brother and his family a few years ago. Was it Miami or Boca?

She jotted down the time code. Later when she went to the studio, she'd check the tape in one of the edit bays. She could zoom in and out and maybe find what she was looking for.

Her cell phone rang and she answered it, hoping it was Terrence's office calling about an interview.

"Hey, it's Josie."

Tory couldn't help but smile. After the long day she'd had, it was nice to finally hear a friendly voice on the phone. "Hey. Did you get my e-mail on Tom King?"

"Yes. If he taught at Athena, and the fertility clinic where his sperm was stored was broken into around the time of Rainy's supposed appendectomy—that's too much for coincidence."

"I agree. We need to make sure that Shannon doesn't get this information. God knows what kind of bizarro story she'd do." Tory didn't want to tell her friends that the Athena story leak to Shannon had been her doing. She felt as if she'd brought a viper into their home and hadn't recognized it for too long.

She wanted revenge against Perry, but a part of her could understand why he'd gone after Shannon. She'd analyzed his action and recognized it as a bid for Tory's attention and love. The two things she'd never really been able to give him.

"She wouldn't have to make much up. Egg mining and stolen sperm—it sounds like a movie of the week on the sci-fi channel."

"I know. What were you calling about?" Tory asked. Not that she didn't like chatting with Josie but she knew that her friend didn't have excess time.

"I traced your surveillance photos, and something

weird was going on down there. Someone came in just as I'd located them. I wasn't able to really analyze the photo and when I went back later it was gone."

"Did you see anything?"

"Yes. A Chinook helicopter took off just as King's team was raiding the camp."

"Wouldn't they have heard it?"

"Not necessarily. I'm betting they were doing air-to-ground backup. The chopper was about ten miles from the base camp."

"My theory is that someone high up was there doing something illegal. What do you think?"

"It's possible. But can you prove anything?"

"Not yet. But I know if I ask the right person the right question I won't have to."

"Who is the right person?"

"I'm not sure. Not yet. You got anything else for me?"

"No. Listen, I heard about Derrick. You okay?"

"Yes. He's recovering," Tory said. She knew she had to warn Josie. "He asked some questions for me, Josie. So watch your back."

"I will. Keep in touch and be careful," Josie said before she hung up.

A knock sounded at the door, and Tory climbed to her feet. "Who is it?"

"Not room service," Ben said.

Tory opened the door. He strode into the room, seeming to fill the large space with his intensity. "Have I got a lead for you."

"Why are you helping me now?"

"Because I don't like the fact that I can't get any answers and something's not adding up. There's only one reporter I trust to cover this story."

"Me?"

"You."

Shivering in the dark and cold on the steps of the Lincoln Memorial, Tory scanned the crowd for Ruben Jimenez, a former Chinook helicopter pilot who had left the service. Military men weren't allowed to talk to the press, and Tory realized how risky this was for Ruben and Ben both. Even though Ruben was retired. Ben was waiting a few blocks away in the car he'd rented. He'd wanted to come, but Tory had insisted that he stay behind.

She'd never needed a man to do her job in the past and she didn't want to start needing Ben now. She clicked on her purse camera.

"Miss Patton?"

Tory turned toward the shadows on the right of the monument and saw a man in his midtwenties. He wore dark jeans, a leather bomber jacket zipped to the throat and a scarf around his neck. His dark hair was close cropped, and his face held a maturity and seriousness that set him apart from his peers.

"Yes. Ruben?"

"Yes, ma'am."

"Thanks for agreeing to meet with me."

He stood stiffly, almost at attention. He scanned the light crowd of people milling up and down the monument stairs. On this chilly November evening not too many were brave enough to actually come out and linger.

"No problem, ma'am. What do you want to know?" he asked. A slight Southern accent tinged his words. He pulled a pack of cigarettes from his pocket and lit one.

"You were a helicopter pilot who flew in Puerto Isla?"

"Yes, ma'am."

"Do you remember what happened during the SEAL mission?" she asked.

He nodded. He clasped his hands behind his back and leaned down toward her. Speaking softly but clearly. "I was on a routine surveillance mission out in a remote location."

He smelled of Old Spice, nicotine and coffee. Tory was wearing heels so she was at least five foot five right now, but he still towered over her. "Do you know who the official was?"

"General Joseph McKinley from army intelligence."

"Did you fly him often?"

"Once a month we took him into the interior. Mostly we were on surveillance, providing air cover for the DEA and CIA guys on the ground who were raiding the ranches."

Interesting. She added this detail to the facts swirling inside her head. "Was this the first time other officials were on your chopper?"

"Yes."

"What happened? Did you get fired on?" Tory wasn't sure she wanted to believe that the government would knowingly send an entire platoon of SEALs to their death and then leave King to be tortured and starved for six months.

"No. I put down a distance from the camp. I let McKinley and his companion off."

"Then what happened?"

"They left and returned a little over an hour later."

"What did the men discuss on the way back?"

"Nothing. I took them back to the city and returned to my base camp."

"When did you leave?"

"Almost immediately. That was my last flight in Puerto Isla. I left the army to come back home and work with my dad."

Tory remembered some basic military information from her time at Athena, but it had been more than a few years. And this situation wasn't a normal military operation. Maybe Ben would be able to lend his military expertise to what she'd found out.

Tory tried to assimilate everything he'd said. Unless she was really off the mark, it sounded as if someone in military intelligence was involved.

"Thanks for speaking to me, Ruben."

"You're welcome, ma'am."

Ruben walked away. Tory waited a few seconds before heading back toward Ben and the waiting car.

She slid into the car and Ben glanced over at her. "Did you find out anything new?"

"Does he work for you?"

"Why do you care?"

"Just curious."

"If he worked for me, he wouldn't be allowed to talk to you."

"Did you know that army intelligence was making trips to the interior of Puerto Isla on a regular basis?"

"No. But I have been asking a few questions back at base."

"And?"

"And Ruben's name turned up."

"I'm really getting angry about this entire mess. Every question I ask leads to more questions. Do you think Addler would know more about this?"

"The embassy and the military work closely together, but I'm not sure what Addler would know."

"I wonder if he'll talk to me again. I want to shake him up."

"Should I drive you there?"

"Ben, I'm a journalist, not an enforcer."

"I'll be your enforcer, babe."

"Don't call me babe. And you've got to do something about those cornball lines."

"It's part of my charm." And he was charming. She realized she was seeing the real Ben, not the suave man who moved through the sophisticated circles of the upper crust. He wasn't wooing her or playing any games with her. And that warmed her deep inside.

Tory warned herself not to fall for it. Ben might be pursuing her with all the intensity of a heat-seeking missile, but he'd lose interest in her soon enough. He was used to the cream of the crop. "Is that how you woo heiresses and heads of state?"

"No. That's all an act that I learned at my mother's knee."

"So what's this?" She gestured to the two of them.

He reached across the space and took her hand in his. "This is the real Ben. Not many people get to see him."

"I'm honored," she said. And deep inside she was.

The light changed and Ben lifted his head. In his eyes she saw the same questions she was battling when it came to this attraction between them. She ran her finger over her bottom lip, not sure what to say. God, the one time she really needed to have words, she didn't.

She fell back as she always did on her career. This story was turning into more than her big break at the UBC. She felt it in her bones. She was uncovering a conspiracy here that was bigger than anyone would believe. The organization of this many different groups.

That meant someone high up, where orders were given that wouldn't be questioned. With the military that meant a high-level officer. But Addler wasn't military and he wasn't talking. So Tory added the diplomatic corps to the mix. And Derrick had been shut down at the DEA.

"Would you drop me off at the network? I want to run these names through our database and see what comes up. And I need to look at a piece of film I shot earlier."

He sighed but let her change the subject. "I'll help you."

"I work better on my own." Which was, strictly speaking, the truth. But she knew she wanted distance from Ben.

"Suit yourself," he said. He was silent the rest of the drive to the studio, and Tory had the insane impulse to apologize.

"I didn't interfere on Puerto Isla when you were giving directions."

Ben pulled the car into a vacant parking lot and put it in Park. He twisted in the seat to face her, one arm resting on the back of the seat, the other bent on the steering wheel. In the shadowed interior of the car, his features were hawklike. She had a feeling that she wouldn't survive a battle with him. He was a warrior now. Not the suave, sophisticated playboy who was at home in Savile Row suits. This was the military expert who'd gotten Tom King off Puerto Isla alive.

A shiver of pure excitement ran down her spine. Going toe-to-toe with him like this…she craved it.

"Like hell you didn't. And I was smart enough to use you and your Athena Academy skills. Even the Amazons teamed up with males once in a while."

"I don't think I'm an Amazon." But she liked that he thought she was. Ben wasn't like other guys she'd been involved with in the past. He came from a family of wealth, privilege and intelligence. She wasn't like the women he socialized with, but she could go toe-to-toe with him on matters like this one.

"I do. And I respect you for that, Tory. I'm not trying to crowd you, but I have as much at stake here as you do."

"How do you figure?" she asked.

"Someone betrayed a special-ops team—I need to avenge that."

"Turning vigilante on me?"

"Not on your life. But we take care of our own problems at LASER."

"What if this isn't a LASER problem?"

"If it concerns any branch of the military, it is. Now, can I come in? Or do you want me to pick you up later?"

"I need you to keep this quiet—can you do that? Let me get the facts and do the story before you go off half-cocked looking for justice."

"First of all, I never go off half-cocked. And second, it depends on what we find. If no one else will be put in danger, I can wait."

"Park in the garage."

"Yes, ma'am."

The network studios weren't that busy. Tory and Ben signed in at the security desk and made their way through the darkened maze of cubicles to the back wall and the one that Tory was using.

"Why don't you use one of the other computers and start searching for information from a year ago forward?" Tory powered up the computer on her desk.

"Why only a year?" Ben asked. He leaned in the doorway, arms crossed over his chest. The blue Oxford shirt he wore under his sport coat that made his eyes even bluer than normal.

"How far back do you think this goes?" she asked after a second. Stop drooling, girl. You're here to do a job, not lust after Ben.

He shrugged and tipped his head to the side. "I'm not sure, but I'm betting for more than a year."

"Okay, five years?" she suggested. She didn't care when he searched as long as he left her alone so she could get to work. Concentrating on Puerto Isla, drug lords and Tom King instead of remembering how it felt to have Ben's big, strong body close to hers.

"Sounds good."

"Did Ruben tell you about McKinely?" she asked, after a minute. She suspected Ruben worked with Ben.

"Yes."

"Does Ruben know who else was with him?"

"Not by name."

"Why didn't you just give me that information?" She didn't know for sure if Ben was working with her or making sure she didn't uncover something that would hurt the image of the military and the U.S. government. And his comments in the car made her wonder whom he'd choose if push came to shove—her or his country.

"Because you notice things that I don't."

"I didn't this time."

"Sure, you did. I wouldn't have connected it to Addler."

"I spoke to Addler this afternoon, and the man was definitely not telling me all he knows."

"That must have ticked you off."

"Ha ha. I don't get ticked off. I just get more curious. I'm not sure Addler's involved with whatever's going on, but he does know more about the hostage incident."

"I'll work him from my end and see what I can find out."

"Thanks, Ben."

"Anything for you."

"Do you mean that?"

"Sure, I do."

"You scare me."

"I know better, Athena girl. Nothing scares you."

He left her alone in the office. Tory turned back to the screen. How little Ben understood about her. Everything scared her. She was afraid she'd endanger someone else with her questions.

Afraid she'd jump into something with Ben that she wasn't ready for.

Chapter 15

Ben pulled into the parking garage at her hotel three hours later. Tory stared at him across the darkened expanse of the front seat. Excitement buzzed through her veins.

She'd called McKinley's office, and she had been informed that McKinley had no comment to the press—especially about Tom King and the SEAL platoon on Puerto Isla. She'd been directed to the army public-affairs office.

"No one in McKinley's office will talk to me," she said to Ben.

"Are you asking me to help out?" he asked.

"Do I really have to ask? You've been butting in since we met on Puerto Isla."

"I thought I was helping."

She sighed. "You have been."

Ben watched her for a minute, then took out his cell phone and made a series of calls. Tory didn't listen in on his conversations. She knew there were some things in Ben's life she was better off not knowing. He'd invited her to join him at a political dinner the next evening with Washington, D.C., insiders who he'd said would probably be able to shed some light on her investigation. Formal dress, lousy food but slow dancing, he'd said. And she was contemplating it.

Idiot, she thought. Once she was seen in public with Ben she could forget about keeping her relationship private. She'd have to call Alex before Alex called her. She didn't want to talk to Alex about Ben. And she didn't want to even contemplate running into Veronica, Ben and Alex's mother. From what she'd heard through Alex, Veronica was a barracuda when it came to the waters of the social dating game. And Tory wasn't sure she was the kind of woman Veronica would want in Ben's life.

"I'm going to meet a McKinley aide for coffee tomorrow morning. I'll see what I can find out."

"Thanks, Ben."

"You're welcome. I love it when you ask me for things."

"Really?"

"Yes."

"Want to come up for a drink?" she asked. They'd

been together the better part of the day, and he'd been on her mind.

"Maybe."

She wasn't in the mood to play games. She opened her door and got out of the car. She was out of her element with him. Give her a reluctant interviewee and she was golden, but one-on-one with this man...she didn't know how to react. Mostly because he never reacted the way he should.

"Hey, where are you going?" he asked.

Tory stood there with the car door open talking into the car. "Up to my room."

"We're in the middle of a conversation."

"No, Ben. We were in the middle of some kind of game. I'm not really interested in playing."

He sighed and rubbed the back of his neck. He was tired. She was, too. And though she'd never admit it, she'd be happy to just lie in Ben's arms for a few hours.

"We need to talk before I come back to your room," he said at last.

"I asked you in for a drink," she said, knowing she'd offered more. "We can go to the bar."

"I want to come up to your room. God, Tory, I want you."

"So what's stopping you?" she asked.

"I think this is more than a few nights of sex here and there."

She wanted it to be more. But with Ben she was afraid to risk caring. He wasn't a guy like Perry who worked in her industry or had any other normal job. Ben did something few men would and he risked his life daily.

"Let's go to the bar. I'm buying."

Ben took her hand and laced their fingers together. Shivers moved up her arm, spreading throughout her body. Once they were in the elevator, she pushed him back against the wall and leaned up against him.

"I don't really want to talk."

She cut off his reply with her mouth against his. He moaned deep in his throat. Sensing victory, she thrust her tongue past his teeth and tasted him. God, he tasted good.

She tunneled her fingers through his thick hair and held his head still. She ravaged his mouth, taking what she wanted without asking.

The door opened and she stepped back. Ben watched her for a moment. When she led him off the elevator across the plush lobby of the hotel to the elevators leading to the guest rooms, he came with her.

"I know I'm going to regret this," he said.

"I promise you won't."

He gave her a half smile that made her heartbeat speed up. "There's regret and then there's regret."

"Don't," she said, covering his lips with her gloved fingers. "Please don't make this into more than…"

"Something physical?"

"Yes."

"Go on up. I need to make a purchase."

She nodded. "Don't be too long."

"I won't be."

She watched him walk away. The elevator car arrived and Tory stepped on. It stopped on the eighth floor and a tall, thin man got on. Tory fixed her on-air smile on her face.

He smiled back at her and the doors to the car closed. Tory glanced down through the glass elevators at the lobby.

He crowded close to her in the car, and Tory tried to back away, but he pulled her back against his body, holding a knife to her throat.

She lifted her foot to kick him, but he tightened his hand on her windpipe and stars danced in front of her eyes. "Be still."

His voice was gruff and barely a whisper. Tory stopped struggling. Her mind shifted through possibilities. She could pretend to faint and pull him off balance then attack him.

She closed her eyes to focus on what she'd do. In her head she visualized the man she'd seen.

"Leave the Puerto Isla matter alone. This is your last warning."

The elevator car stopped again. The man released her and walked off the elevator. Tory started after him, but the doors closed before she could get off the car.

Tory wasn't in her room five minutes before there was a knock on the door. She approached the door, cautiously aware that someone could fire through it and kill her.

"It's Ben."

She checked the peephole and then opened the door. His coat was torn, his eye was starting to turn black and his nose was bloodied. "What happened to you?"

"Got in a little tussle with some friends of yours," he said with a cocky grin that said he'd gotten the best of his opponent.

He wiped his nose with the back of his hand. Tory pulled him into the room and closed the door. This was getting out of hand. She needed to finish this story so that she could get back to living a normal life. So that the people who she came in contact with were no longer in danger.

"Go sit down. I had a warning also."

She wet one of the washcloths with cold water and brought another one with her. She wrapped some ice in the dry cloth. "Hold this on the back of your neck."

He looked skeptical. "My nose is bleeding, Tory."

She forced his hand against the back of his neck. "I know. But this works. My brother used to get nose-bleeds when we were kids. Mom always put ice on the back of his neck."

He tilted his head to one side. "I don't know anything about your family, but your mom sounds a whole lot different from mine."

"I think it's safe to say she is. She's a ranch wife, so she's very practical and down-to-earth."

"Are you close?"

Tory thought about it for a minute. She talked to her mom practically every day. "Yes, we are. She's just wise and supportive. And she doesn't nag or say 'I told you so.'"

"Like my grandfather."

"How does he feel about you 'wasting your life'?"

"He understands."

"How could he? He was the director of the CIA, Ben. The man has to want you to do more with your life." Tory couldn't imagine having to live up to a man like Charles Forsythe. He was bigger than life. A millionaire many times over, but also a man of integrity and honor.

"Trust me, Tory. He's not upset with me."

"Why not?" she asked. She was probably right to suspect that his grandfather knew the truth about Ben.

"Let it go," he said.

"I can't. You got the journalist in me stirred up." She thought about Alex and Ben's dad, who'd died when they were young. Alex didn't often speak of her father, but Tory pulled the memory of a long-ago chat. Alex's dad had died overseas on a business trip. Overseas in a dangerous area, Tory remembered, because they'd been studying hot spots around the world and how the State Department decided which countries to warn American citizens against traveling to. "Does it have something to do with your dad?"

Ben stiffened. "How the hell did you do that?"

She smiled. She was good at connecting the dots. "Let's see. He ran an import-export business and died on a business trip in…Turkey?"

"Yes."

"He was CIA like your grandfather, right?"

"I'm not sure, but I think so."

"Didn't your grandfather tell you?"

"We've never talked about it. But there's a plaque on the wall at the CIA headquarters for a fallen operative and the date matches when Dad…"

Tory hugged him tight to her. It seemed the Forsythe men had a history of fighting for their country though no one else would ever know.

She didn't want to talk about families. She didn't want to give herself or him the illusion that what they had would last longer than it took to air this story.

"What about your family? Any secrets hidden there?"

"Nope. I grew up on a ranch in Florida. My brother and I roamed all over like we owned the world."

"Are you close to your brother?" he asked, dropping her hand.

"Yes, Derrick and I are very close. But that's because of my folks—mostly my mom. She's always calling us and making us call each other."

"Sounds…nice." Ben closed his eyes.

Tory dabbed a little more at his nose. She didn't want to hurt him. And his face looked pretty bad. "You could be closer to Alex if you came clean. She's trustworthy, you know."

"I know. But she's not a very good liar."

"That's not a bad thing."

"It could be for my cover. Right now Alex plays a big part in that. She's so exasperated with the man I am supposedly that no one thinks to look beyond that image."

"I never did," Tory admitted. But having seen the real man now, she knew she'd never be fooled by his apathetic man-about-town image again.

"And you're no dummy."

"Wow, watch out with all those compliments—you might turn my head."

He ran one finger down the side of her face. She tipped her head into his hand. "It'd take more than words to turn your head."

"You think so?" She wasn't sure what it took. Her relationship skills weren't that great. For a minute she was reminded of Perry's betrayal and she felt that maybe she wasn't as smart about people as she'd always imagined she was.

"I know so. You're a tough character, Tory Patton."

"Ha. Not hardly."

"You intimidate everyone you meet. I think you know it and like it."

She thought about what he'd said. Ben was more insightful than she had given him credit for being. "Maybe I do. But I'm short so I have a lot to make up for."

She cleaned his nose and applied pressure to stem

the bleeding. Ben wrapped his free arm around her waist and pulled her down on his lap. He tossed the ice-filled washcloth into the ice bucket. And pushed her hand off his face.

"Who delivered your warning?"

"A guy with a knife on the elevator."

"I had two thugs with brass knuckles. I'm supposed to warn you that if you don't stop asking questions they're going to kill you."

"I'm sorry, Ben."

"Don't be." He ran his thumb along her bottom lip.

"Are you going to heed their advice?"

"Hell, no. If I knew who they were, I wouldn't have to ask any more questions."

"Are you sure you want to pursue this? It's getting dangerous."

Tory thought about it for a minute, but in her mind nothing had really changed. This story wasn't just about her career anymore. It was about truth and honor. Two things that she had feeling the person behind her threats knew nothing about. "I'm not giving up."

"What is in that water at Athena Academy?" he asked in an exasperated tone.

Ben had a chip on his shoulder about Athena. Why? "The same thing that's in the water you drank. Would you give up?"

"That's different. I'm a trained operative."

"So am I."

"I know it. Listen, I've got to get out of here. I want

to check in with Ruben and make sure he wasn't followed."

"Okay. Call after you talk with McKinley's aide. I finally got an appointment with Terrence for tomorrow." She'd gotten confirmation earlier when they were at the network.

"Terrence?"

"Paul Terrence. He is the current U.S. drug czar."

"Be careful, Tory."

"Hey, I always am."

Ben walked out the door. Tory put the night chain on and went to bed, trying not to be sorry that the night had ended this way instead of as she'd planned. Making notes and pursuing her story was enough to keep her busy tonight. She didn't miss the man who'd just left her. Not one little bit.

Tory woke at 6:00 a.m. when her phone rang. She stretched her arm for the receiver. She'd ordered a wake-up call after Ben left. Today she was going to get some answers. No matter who she had to hound to find them.

"Hello," she said.

"Tory Patton?"

"Yes, who is this?"

"Don't worry about that. I have some information for you. Some of Whitlow's campaign funding came from the Puerto Isla coca-leaf farmers."

"What?"

"Track it down and see for yourself."

"Who is this?"

"An interested third party."

"Can we meet and discuss this?"

"No."

The caller hung up. Tory rubbed the sleep from her eyes. She got out of bed and got dressed. Campaign contributions could be the missing puzzle piece to explain why it had taken so long to rescue Tom. If Whitlow was taking a kick-back from Puerto Isla, then he probably had promised to keep the DEA and military out of the country. But was it Whitlow who'd taken the money and made the deal, or someone close to him? Did the president of the United States have knowledge about those events? It left a lot of information in the that gray area between what was right and wrong.

She called Ben on the cell number he'd left her, but only got his voice mail. "It's Tory, call me."

She dressed with care, making sure that every hair was on-air perfect. She'd brought an entire suitcase of power suits with her. You couldn't come to D.C. and not dress appropriately. This place had been founded on tradition, and flouting that tradition wouldn't open the doors she needed to have opened.

She wasn't sure what to make of her early-morning wake-up call. Still trying to determine if it was just a crackpot with an agenda against Whitlow, Tory got out of her cab at Paul Terrence's office at ten minutes to nine.

A woman in her early twenties arrived next. She didn't invite Tory to wait inside. Tory didn't mind. Her wool overcoat was a good one, and she scarcely noticed the chilly November air.

Security was tight at the building, which was what had taken so long for her to get the interview. Everyone who entered the building had to be cleared.

A black sedan pulled up twenty minutes later. A couple of U.S. marshals got out of the car and escorted Terrence into the building. Tory waited until he was inside before she herself entered.

Paul Terrence didn't really look like his press photo from the Internet. He wasn't as tall as she'd expected him to be. He'd probably been an attractive man at some point, but he'd started putting on weight around the middle and his hair was thinning.

She entered the building and gave her name at the security desk. She was searched and sent up for her appointment.

She arrived in the office of the National Drug Control Policy and had to wait another fifteen minutes before Terrence was ready to see her.

She was escorted to his office by his personal assistant. Terrence's office had an American flag in one corner. The decor was very masculine, all dark woods and big chairs.

"Hello, Mr. Terrence. I'm Tory Patton with UBC."

"Good morning, Ms. Patton. Please have a seat, and call me Paul."

"Thank you, sir. Call me Tory," she said. Most people would be comfortable in the guest chair, but Tory was petite and felt as if she were being swallowed by it.

She perched on the end of her chair, ready to ask her questions. The wall held the usual assortment of framed pictures, a Harvard degree and a few awards. Tory skimmed her gaze over the pictures, not really observing, but preserving them in her mind.

"Can I offer you some coffee?"

"No, thanks. Since you are pressed for time I'd rather get to it and ask you some questions."

"Of course. How can I help you?"

"How familiar are you with the hostage situation on Puerto Isla earlier this year in which Tom King and his SEAL team were ambushed?"

"Just what I've heard you report. Very nice work, by the way."

Flattery, how nice. Too bad she wasn't buying it. She knew she shouldn't be in this office asking questions.

She'd been warned, her brother had been shot and the person whom she'd made nervous wasn't in the mood to play games. Terrence might or might not have knowledge of the illegal campaign contributions. But whoever did might get wind of this interview and then she'd be in hot water…again.

She wasn't sure which questions she should be asking. "Is the coca-leaf eradication process moving more smoothly there now that Alejandro Del Torro has taken office?"

"I believe so. I think you should speak to our public-affairs office. We put out a press release just last week on Puerto Isla. But I believe the program has been successful. We're hoping to mirror the operation and results we had in Peru."

"Have you been to Puerto Isla?"

"No."

"Has anyone from your office?"

"What are you getting at, Ms. Patton?"

"Nothing," she said. She realized she might have overstepped her boundaries by coming here. Had she made a mistake?

"I heard some disturbing rumors when I was on the island last week about Del Torro being involved in coca-leaf farming."

"We're aware of that. If he doesn't stay in line with our policies, we'll be forced to stop all financial aid to Puerto Isla. You've been there, so you know firsthand how desperately they need our government's help."

"Yes, I do. Why is our government backing Del Torro if he's in the coca-leaf business?"

"He's the lesser of two evils."

Terrence's phone rang and he reached for the handset. He listened for a minute and then lifted his gaze to Tory. "If that's all…? I have a call I need to take."

"Of course. Thanks for your time."

Tory left his office and was escorted back to the elevators, and she knew she was watched until she left the building. What had Terrence told her? Nothing, she thought. The same as Addler the day before.

She lifted her arm to hail a taxi. She gave them the address for the UBC studios in D.C. She wanted to check out McKinley, Terrence, Addler, Whitlow, Del Torro and Pearson and see if there was a connection anywhere.

She also needed to go through Whitlow's campaign contributions and see where the money came from.

Chapter 16

Tory spent the rest of the day on the Internet and talking to contacts. Whitlow's campaign funding was a spreadsheet that was a mile long and had more entries than she could keep straight. So far she hadn't found a connection to Puerto Isla.

It was almost lunchtime on Tuesday and she still hadn't heard from Ben. She wasn't going to worry about him. He could take care of himself. Telling herself that didn't stop the bad feeling she had in the pit of her stomach.

The phone rang and she answered it. "UBC, Tory Patton speaking."

"Hi, sweetie."

"Hi, Mom. How's Derrick?"

Tory could hear the radio playing in the background. She pictured her mom standing in the kitchen of their big ranch house probably making sandwiches for lunch. "Much better. He's out of the hospital. Dad went to pick up his family and bring them to the house for Thanksgiving. Will you be able to break away and join us?"

Since it was Tuesday and her story was finally coming together, Tory doubted it. "I don't think so."

Her mom made that sound that always indicated she was disappointed in Tory. "Mom, I've got enough guilt going on about what happened to Derrick. Please don't make me feel guilty about not coming for Thanksgiving. I promise I'll take two weeks off at Christmas and come home."

"Sweetie, making you feel guilty is my job. And if you ever get married, nagging you about giving me grandchildren will be my chief focus."

She laughed. God, she missed her family. She'd love to be on her way to the airport and then on her way home. Feeling her parents' love and support. But the tingling feeling in her gut warned that time was of the essence and leaving now might mean missing out on an important detail. And if someone was gunning for her, she didn't want to be anywhere near her family.

"Thanks, Mom."

"For what?"

"Just being you."

"You're welcome, sweetie. If you need us you know where we are."

"I'll call on turkey day."

Her mom hung up and Tory leaned back in her chair. She reached for her cup of tea and found that it had grown cold. She went to the break room to get another cup. The television, which was tuned to UBC's all-day news station flashed a photo of the Potomac River. The news ticker at the bottom said an unidentified man's body had been pulled from the river that morning.

The footage was grainy and not close enough to identify anything about the body. Tory prayed it wasn't Ben. Why would it be? But the warnings she'd been given lately lingered in her mind.

Tory went down the hall to the newsroom. Marsha Cranston, a forty-five-year-old with the kind of news experience Tory hoped to have at her age, sat behind her big desk. Marsha monitored all news wires, as well as the other networks to see what they were running. "Did they identify that John Doe they pulled out of the Potomac yet?"

"Our sources haven't, but apparently ABS has."

"Who was it?" Tory asked, heart in her throat.

"I don't know. Shannon Conner is doing a report on it right now."

Tory leaned over the desk, and Marsha handed her a pair of earphones. "A former army helicopter pilot's body was pulled from the Potomac River early this morning. Ruben Jimenez left the military earlier this year after serving in Central America. I'll have an exclusive interview with Ruben's father and fiancée on tonight's evening news. This is Shannon Conner, broadcasting live from Washington, D.C."

Tory handed the earphones back to Marsha. Her stomach felt tight and bile rose in the back of her throat. Had she caused Ruben's death? Of course she had. It was too much to be just a coincidence.

She knew she needed to figure out the clues in this damned story before anyone else died. She was glad she'd decided not to go home for Thanksgiving.

Her phone was ringing when she entered her office. Tory stared at it for a minute, afraid to pick up. But she'd never been a quitter and she was pissed off. Whoever was behind this mess was going down. "Patton here."

"It's Ben. I've got some bad news."

"Is it about Ruben?" she asked. Oh, thank God he was okay. She didn't dwell on it. Didn't want to spend too much time thinking about the feelings that had flooded her when she'd first heard his voice. He was just a guy she knew. There was no emotional connection between them.

But the frantic beating of her heart said otherwise.

"You know?" he asked, his normally deep voice even more gruff than usual.

"I just saw it on TV." She thought about Ruben as she'd last seen him and said a prayer for his soul. Not sure if Rainy could really hear or not, she asked her old friend to watch out for this man who'd helped her at the cost of his life.

"Don't leave the network until I come and pick you up."

"I don't want a bodyguard." Tory knew the only way to get this story done was to stay alone. To keep anyone else from getting involved. She didn't know how she'd find answers on her own, but she'd do it. She wasn't going to risk anyone else's life.

"Too damned bad. I'm taking you to Middleburg until after the Thanksgiving weekend. We can work from there."

"I don't want to go to Forsythe Farms."

"I'm not asking, Tory," he said, and there was a steely tone in his voice she'd never heard before.

Tory wanted to go with Ben. She needed to think, and to do that she needed to feel safe. And D.C. didn't feel safe anymore. "What am I going to tell Alex?"

"That we ran into each other in D.C. and I invited you down for the holiday."

"I don't want to put your family in danger, Ben."

"You won't. No one will follow us and even if they do, there's enough security around that place to keep out the National Guard."

She reluctantly agreed and made arrangements to meet Ben in less than an hour's time in the lobby of the network. Tory sent an e-mail to Tyson Bedders advising him of the progress she'd made and telling him she'd be available via her cell phone.

* * *

Ruben Jimenez's face kept flashing through her mind. She was responsible for his death. Granted, he'd decided to talk to her, but she'd known that danger was stalking her.

"Ready?" Ben asked from her doorway.

"Yes. I need to go by the hotel and pick up my suitcase."

"I already did."

"Should I say thanks?"

"I should think so."

She smiled at Ben, happier to see him than she'd ever admit. His lightness relieved part of the burden in her heart.

Forsythe Farms was nestled in the middle of Virginia horse country. Tory leaned back against her seat and closed her eyes as Ben drove. She still wasn't sure coming home with Ben on Thanksgiving was such a great idea.

Maybe because it felt right in her soul. That secret place she'd hidden and protected so well in other relationships. But with Ben she seemed to have no barrier. She suspected it was because of the circumstances of their meeting.

She warned herself not to place too much importance on this. And he was sticking around due to some kind of…what? She knew he didn't feel brotherly toward her.

"You're quiet. Should I be scared?" Ben asked as they drove west on I-495.

She turned her head on the seat rest to look at him. They'd left D.C. in the middle of the afternoon. Traffic had been heavy, but Ben had maneuvered his way through it with his usual skill.

"No."

He drove in silence as they turned onto Route 50. Tory watched the dappled sunlight filter through the trees and felt some of the tension lingering in her gut ease. This was a great day to be alive. She reached across the expanse of the two seats and settled her hand on Ben's thigh.

Thankfully he said nothing, only lowered his big, warm hand on top of hers. The facts of the story she was investigating ran through her head with dizzying speed, and she knew that if she could just let everything settle down for a day she'd be able to put it together.

"Who will be at your grandfather's for the holiday?" she asked at last. She suspected Alex would be there. But she wasn't sure if the Forsythes had a big dinner party.

"Just the family. Grandfather, my mother, Alex and her new beau, Justin Cohen."

"I haven't met him yet." Alex had met Justin while seeking answers about Rainy's death.

Justin had been looking for answers, too—about why his sister had died twenty years ago after agreeing to be a surrogate mother. Around the same time they suspected that Rainy's eggs had been mined and Thomas King's sperm had been stolen. They had no proof, but all the Cassandras believed Justin's sister had probably carried Rainy's child. Hospital records said the baby had died, too, but they were all beginning to wonder.

"I have. He's a good guy. Just the right kind of man for Alex. He works for the FBI, too."

Like all the Cassandras, Alex was doing all she could to figure out what was going on with Rainy's eggs and who had killed Rainy.

"What will we tell Alex?" Tory asked. Years as a television journalist, and she blurted that question out as if she were a rookie.

"About what?" he asked, lifting one eyebrow at her.

Was she acting like a idiot about Ben? Was she making a mountain out of a molehill?

"Tory?"

She shrugged. "About…us."

A mile or so passed before Ben responded. "Nothing. She's my little sister, not my keeper."

"She's also one of my best friends." Which was what really bothered her. Normally Tory would have called Alex the minute she'd arrived in D.C. Instead she'd been wary of talking to her old friend. Afraid she'd somehow reveal Ben's secret.

"Don't sweat the details, Tory. Everyone will think I charmed you." His tone was light and she knew he was trying to reassure her.

She decided to let him for now. She'd been friends with Alex too long to let anything come between them.

"I've seen your version of charm—we should both be sweating."

He lifted her hand from his thigh and kissed the back of it, then smiled and drove on, seemingly unaffected.

He executed a series of turns that brought them to Forsythe Farms. Ben made the turn into the drive and stopped at the security gate. He got a remote and pressed a series of numbers into it. The gate slid open and he drove through.

He waited for the gate to close again before continuing on to the house. She'd never thought about the security precautions that must be implicit in being Charles Forsythe's grandchildren. "Was it restrictive?"

"Was what?"

"Growing up with this kind of security."

"No. Actually I think these circumstances are partially responsible for the way I live."

"How?"

"Grandfather made life so normal and yet at the same time taught us safety skills. It just feels right to live two lives—to blend two very different lifestyles."

He shrugged and she knew she'd get him to say no more. But she understood exactly what he meant. Another piece of the puzzle that was Bennington Forsythe slipped into place.

Ben pulled to a stop in the circular drive. Alex's Lexus SUV was parked in the driveway, and Tory's hands began to sweat.

Her reaction was ridiculous. She knew Alex

wouldn't be bothered that Tory was dating her brother. "Are we dating?"

"Trying to figure out what to tell Alex?"

"Yes."

Ben leaned across the seat and cupped her jaw. "Tell her you enchanted me."

"I thought your other persona didn't have corny lines."

"That's not corny. It's romantic."

"Are you going to sit in the car all day or are you coming inside?" Charles Forsythe asked as he opened Ben's car door.

The Forsythes were very warm and welcoming. Of course, Tory knew the family through Alex. And their grandfather Charles had been one of the founders of Athena Academy. Alex had greeted her enthusiastically when she and Ben had walked into the house, but they hadn't had a chance to talk.

Alex looked happy with Justin Cohen. More than happy. Her eyes glowed with an inner warmth that Tory had never seen in her friend before.

Justin's intensity reminded her of Ben. Another powerful male presence. They were all in the dinner room eating a light supper. Charles sat at the head of the table, Alex on his left and Ben on his right. Tory sat next to Ben, and Justin next to Alex. Veronica was at the far end.

Tory and Ben still wore the clothes they'd traveled

in. Tory had on a pair of camel-colored trousers and a black sweater. Veronica was going to a party in D.C. later on so she was dressed for an evening out. Alex, as always, looked classy.

"How was Miami, Ben?" Alex asked when they'd all settled at the table to eat dinner.

Tory tipped her head to glance at Ben. She remembered their meeting on Puerto Isla and knew that if she and Ben remained a couple she'd never be able to share that story with anyone. Ben winked at her in that sly way of his.

"Fun. You can't beat the warm weather and sun-tanned beauties on Florida's Gold Coast. I stayed with some friends of yours, Mother."

"The Bentons. Did you get on well with Amanda? She'd make an excellent daughter-in-law," Veronica said, without sparing a glance for Tory.

Ben squeezed her leg under the table. "Now, Mother, you know I never kiss and tell…but I think you'd be disappointed with Amanda."

"I doubt that," Veronica said. Tory knew from Alex that Veronica wanted her offspring married and married well.

"How did you two hook up?" Alex asked.

Tory could only stare at her friend. She knew that Ben wasn't supposed to have been on Puerto Isla, so she wasn't sure what to say. She glanced at Ben.

"We met in the Miami airport. I was my usual charming self and she couldn't resist me."

"Ha. Have you heard the corny lines he uses? I'm beginning to think Bennington Forsythe, legendary lover, is a child's bedtime story."

There was a moment of silence and Tory rubbed the back of her neck. Maybe she shouldn't have said something that might lead the others to investigate Ben's supposed jet-setting.

"Do you see the abuse I have to put up with?" Ben asked. Wearing jeans and a Nordic sweater, he didn't look like his playboy image. And here with his family he was at ease. She noticed he was careful to not let any subject get too weighty and hardly five minutes went by without Ben making some kind of joke or teasing comment.

"Big bro, you always have thought you were too slick for your own good."

"Hey, what'd I do to deserve this abuse? Grandpa, help me out here."

"You did it to yourself, my boy." Charles wore a pleased expression. Tory sensed he was happy to have both his grandchildren back under his roof.

Dinner continued with lots of ribbing. Even Veronica was teased by both of her children about a man who was interested in her. Tory enjoyed seeing this side of both Alex and Ben.

Dinner ended and Veronica left to go to the party. Alex and Justin went for a walk and Tory found herself alone with two enigmas. She saw a lot of Charles in Ben.

"Can we speak in your study?" Ben asked his grandfather.

"Go ahead. I have to make a call and I'll join you."

Tory followed Ben down the hall and into the book-shelf-lined room. Tory walked in and stood for a moment to absorb the old-world elegance of the room.

"I think you should tell my grandfather what you have, Tory. He'll be able to add some insight."

Tory bit her lip, undecided. She didn't want Ben or Charles taking over the Puerto Isla matter. She'd wanted to figure it out on her own. God, she was whining, she thought. Charles Forsythe had been in the Washington intelligence community for a long time. Tory would be a fool not to ask him for some advice.

The door opened and Charles walked into the room. Tory and Ben were still standing a foot apart watching each other. Tory nodded to Ben.

"Anyone want a drink?" Charles asked.

"I'll take a Scotch," Ben said.

"I'll have something sweet."

Charles fixed them both drinks, as well as one for himself. Tory took a sip of her liquor and found it to be amaretto. She knew the drink was one of Alex's favorites. She closed her eyes and forgot for a minute that she was in Ben's family home. She concentrated on the fact that this was also the home of one of her Athena sisters. She remembered how, when they'd all first arrived at Athena, they'd been too competitive with each other to accomplish anything.

Rainy had tricked them into putting their differences aside. Individually they were all powerful women, but together…together they were awesome.

Tory knew that Rainy was reminding her that sometimes she had to ask for help to find the answers she was seeking.

"I could use your advice," Tory said. Ben took her arm and seated her on the leather love seat.

"What kind of advice?" Charles asked, sitting down on one of the winged green leather armchairs.

"Tory's chasing a story that keeps getting more complicated. I'm working the military angle and she's doing the political thing, but we're missing something. And you dabble in both, so…"

"What have you got?"

Tory recapped everything she'd learned from Tom King, Ruben Jimenez, Dave Addler and Paul Terrence. "Ben spoke to General McKinley's aide. He made several trips to the interior of Puerto Isla, and on the night the SEAL team went in to rescue the hostages, McKinley and another U.S. official were on the island and had just left the scene. And I got an anonymous tip on the phone advising me to check into Whitlow's campaign contributions. I'm not sure what I'm looking for. I have a huge printout of everyone who contributed to his campaign, but I feel like I'm following the chaos theory and searching for the top quark."

"What did McKinley's aide say?" Charles asked Ben.

"Just that McKinley was aware that Tory was asking questions and that I should advise her to stop."

"How did they put us together?" Tory asked.

"They knew I was in D.C. with you. They are also aware that you and Alex are friends from Athena."

"Does this involve Athena Academy?" Charles asked.

"No. Not that I've been able to tell. Though King, Ben and I are all connected to the school."

"Addler, Terrence, Whitlow and McKinley," Charles murmured, sitting back in his chair. Tory ran the names through her head, as well.

The men had nothing in common. Or did they?

In her mind she replayed her interviews with Addler and Terrence. Their offices had been similar. As had the pictures on the wall.

She'd seen pictures of both men on a fishing boat with Chris Pearson, Whitlow's campaign manager.

Chapter 17

"Mr. Forsythe, do you know Chris Pearson?" Tory asked. Thankfully her photographic memory was pulling details about the man that she normally wouldn't have recalled. She'd seen his face on *Fortune* magazine last summer and she remembered reading an article on him in the *Wall Street Journal* just the past week.

Ben froze and glanced at her as if she'd just said something that she wasn't supposed to know. With his eyes narrowed he looked like a predator. Tory shivered and scooted a few inches away from him on the love seat. He did nothing to stop her.

"Yes, I've met the man. Why?"

Ben continued to watch her. She wondered if she'd made a mistake in trusting him. He was a dangerous man. She knew that she'd seen him in action. Plus he was capable of lying to those he loved and doing it convincingly.

Charles watched her, waiting for a response. "I think he might be the link."

"The link between the men?"

"Yes. Well, Jimenez is linked to McKinley because he was the pilot. And McKinley and Addler were both in Puerto Isla at the same time."

"Terrence and McKinley would have some contact with each other through the Pentagon. But why did you bring up Pearson?"

"I saw him in the presidential palace when I first got to Puerto Isla. After that my contact, Juan Perez, denied me access to King. I was thinking of my early-morning caller and his tip that drug money was linked to Whitlow's campaign. There were pictures in both Addler's and Terrence's office of each of them on a fishing boat with Pearson."

"That's weak, Tory," Ben said at last.

Tory knew it was weak and that she was stretching. Was she chasing something that didn't exist? Was she so hungry for a breaking story that she'd follow clues that led to nothing?

Charles leaned back, propping his elbows on the arms of his chair. Ben's grandfather was renowned for being one of the smartest men in the world. He'd been the director of the CIA, and Tory knew it took a certain keen understanding of human nature to have survived as long as he had in that job. Charles nodded slightly at her.

Ben, however, didn't seem as supportive of her ideas. He shifted forward in his seat. "I don't think we should pursue this line of reasoning."

"Why not, Ben?" Tory asked.

He said nothing for a minute, and she reminded herself that this man had depths she'd never really be able to explore. A shiver moved down her spine, and she shifted away from his touch.

"I've been ordered to discourage you from going in this direction."

Charles lowered his hands and stared at them both. "Are you on a black-bag operation?"

Ben didn't respond. Tory had heard the term before. She knew it was some kind of government-okayed killing assignment. Simultaneously she was scared and furious. Scared, because Ben was a trained killer and she'd seen him in action on Puerto Isla. But furious because she must be onto something solid if Ben had been ordered to keep an eye on her. And he'd never confirmed any of it.

Tory stood and moved to the other side of the room. She wanted to punch Ben. Why had he connected her with Jimenez, if he was supposed to keep her from discovering the truth?

"For God's sake, Tory, I'm not going to kill you."

Tory said nothing, only watched the man who was the brother of her best friend. The man who'd made her feel safe at a time when there was danger all around. She believed he wouldn't kill her. Besides, if he'd wanted to, he could have several times on Puerto Isla.

She was ticked off that he'd known all the time. Had he been trying to derail her? She focused only on her investigation and not on Ben.

"Why did you give me Jimenez to interview?"

He wouldn't look at her.

"To gain my trust, right?"

He shrugged.

Damn the man. She tightened her hands into fists. "I'm right to suspect Pearson of being involved, aren't I?"

"Yes," Ben said.

Charles steepled his fingers again. Ben sat back and watched his grandfather. Finally Charles lowered his arms. "We need a plan, young lady."

"I was thinking I'd go to his office and interview him. He was on the news last week. Isn't he managing Whitlow's reelection campaign for next year? Maybe I can use that angle."

"Yes. Do you think he'll buy it?"

"I don't know. Ben, how much do they know about me?"

"I'm not sure. This isn't my usual type of mission. I'm a search-and-retrieve guy. But because of my connection to you through Alex, I was ordered to watch you and see if any names came up. If they did, I was to divert you."

"How?"

"With my charm," he said with a sardonic smile. Oh God. Had he been faking all along?

"That's putting a lot of pressure on your supposed charm."

"They don't think so."

"Was Pearson the only name?"

"No. Addler, Terrence and Whitlow were also on the list."

Something about the way he said it made her believe there were other names on Ben's list. "Who else?"

He shrugged.

She understood that he was under orders. Mentally she made plans to go back to D.C. tonight. She couldn't stay and compromise the Forsythe family. She wasn't backing down from this story.

She searched her mind and made a connection that should have been made earlier. "Del Torro and Santiago."

Ben said nothing and his expression gave away little, but she saw his pupils widen and his nostrils flare as if he were sensing danger.

Well, she had the connection now. Money had been donated to Whitlow's campaign. She had guessed who had given it and why. She also understood why King was better off dead than in prison. If he had seen McKinley and someone else on the island—she was betting on Pearson. He wasn't a government official, but he had enough clout to influence those who worked for the U.S. government. He could also make deals that sounded as if they were coming from Whitlow.

"Charles, do you know Pearson well enough to get me an interview with him?"

Charles hesitated. "Ben, perhaps you should leave. I don't want to compromise your mission."

"I'm not going anywhere. I'm sticking to Tory's side."

"That probably isn't wise."

"Too bad. I originally got involved not knowing all the parameters of this mission. Special ops were betrayed, Grandpa. That could have been my team. And Tory is becoming important to me."

Tory wasn't sure she liked Ben labeling her as his. But deep inside she felt a little reassured that he had. His gaze met hers and he stared into her eyes with an intensity that made her tremble. An intensity that seemed to say, "You belong to me and I protect my own."

It didn't matter that she knew she could protect herself. It didn't matter that every time she trusted a man he let her down. It didn't matter that Ben lied to everyone he cared about. In that instant, she knew he had her.

Charles cleared his throat. "I don't know him well enough to get either of you an appointment. But I believe Veronica socializes with Lydia Pearson."

Ben glanced at her, and Tory wasn't sure what to do. She knew he had a stake in the outcome. But she was used to going it alone. And this time she didn't want him by her side. She couldn't be sure whether he was going along for justice for special ops or to shut her up if she learned too much.

Charles called Veronica, who was en route to her party. Tory didn't take her eyes off Ben. He watched her, as well, and she knew that their relationship would be changed by the outcome of their interview with Pearson.

Her career and her personal life once again were on a collision course. She only hoped that this time her judgment was better than it had been with Perry.

Tory stood in front of the window, staring down at the rolling hills of Virginia. The moon played over the landscape, giving it that dreamy sepia tone that she loved. She longed to have her favorite Nikon in hand. When she was behind the lens of a camera she could forget about her problems and just shoot film.

A light snow started to fall, and Tory was entranced by it. She loved to watch the snow. She didn't get upset by the traffic snarls it inevitably caused or by the wetness it left behind. She'd spent too many Florida winters praying to see it.

She wore a pair of flannel-lined satin pajamas but she still felt chilled. Hugging her arms around herself, she turned away from the window.

She finally had the kind of exclusive story lead she'd always craved, and now she was worried about whether she could do it justice.

Athena Academy training had given each of its graduates that innate knowledge that she could do anything. Take on anyone and come out the winner. But tonight, in Charles Forsythe's study, she hadn't really felt that she could take on anything. She'd felt she might have bitten off more than she could chew.

Honestly, though, was it the story or the situation that bothered her? She'd proved herself on Puerto Isla and had more confidence in her survival skills than ever before. No, what worried her was Bennington Forsythe.

She'd retreated upstairs to type up her notes and write the story that was in her head. The story that she knew was going to rock the capital when she broke it wide open. She'd gone back over the campaign finances and still hadn't found anything concrete to link Del Torro or Santiago, who both were coca-leaf ranchers, to Whitlow.

She knew she was missing something, and hoped that once she talked to Pearson she'd have what she needed to go live with the story.

She was too restless to sleep. She doubted she'd really be able to rest until after this entire story had aired and steps were taken to make sure that no one in Whitlow's White House could willingly hurt U.S. citizens again. She knew that it was a naive attitude, but she clung to it.

There was a brief knock on the bedroom door. "Who is it?"

"Ben. Can I come in?"

"Yes."

He opened the door and paused in the darkened entryway. The light from the hall spilled into the room, and Tory stood where she was, observing him. He wore only a pair of black pajama pants that rode low on his hips. His sleek muscles were illuminated and she just stared at him. Physically he was perfection. Honed, toned and ready for action, he was one of America's fighting elite. And she knew he'd do his job under any circumstances.

"Come to make sure I haven't leaked any state secrets?"

He cursed under his breath and stepped into the room, closing the door behind him. The room was plunged into darkness save for the fall of moonlight in front of the big window.

"Scared?" he asked, in a raspy tone she hadn't heard from him before.

"Bennington Forsythe, Athena women aren't scared of mortals."

"Tory?"

Tory knew it was childish, but she slunk deeper into the shadowy drapes near the window. He walked silently into the room.

After the way he'd scared her earlier, she wanted back a little of her own. She made him come to her, using her own retreat to move him just where she wanted him.

"What kind of game are you playing?" he asked, his voice a husky whisper.

"One where I'm in control."

"I love it when you take control."

"Good."

He crept closer to her and she stood her ground, watching him move. When he was close enough to touch, she reached out and swept him off his feet with a hook kick behind the knees. He controlled his fall, making sure they both landed on the bed.

Tory braced her hands on his shoulders and straddled his waist. He wasn't breathing heavily and neither was she. Well, okay, she was a little bit, but only because he was close to her.

She felt his erection through the layers of both of their pajama pants. "Is this what you had in mind?"

She didn't want to talk. She didn't want to let him get to her any more than he already had. She wasn't going to take him with her to visit Pearson.

She leaned down and nipped his pectoral with her teeth. He moaned deep in his throat, his hips lifting toward hers. She slid down his chest, kissing and nipping.

He caressed her breasts, cupping the full globes in his hands and then lightly scraping her nipple with his nails. He pushed her top up and grabbed her waist, pulling her up his body.

Leaning up, he caught the tip of her nipple between his lips and suckled. She held his head to her body and ground her center against him. She couldn't wait any longer. She had to have him.

She pulled her top off and tossed it on the floor, then reached between them and pushed his pants down his legs. He did the same with hers and in a minute they were pressed body to naked body. His skin was hot to the touch, and everywhere her hands fondled soon grew even warmer.

"Enough," he said between clenched teeth. "There's a condom in the pocket of my pants." Tory reached for his pants and found the condom and quickly covered him with it.

She positioned herself over him and slowly lowered herself down on his length. Ben lay beneath her, coiled and powerful, ready to take command yet letting her have the power. She rode him, swiftly bringing them both to the edge of climax. He grabbed her hips in an iron grasp and thrust upward once and then twice quickly. She shattered and fell over the edge, collapsing on his chest as his shout of completion filled the room.

Alex and Justin were in the sunroom when Tory came downstairs the next morning. Tory hesitated in the doorway, very conscious of the fact that were a lot of things left unsaid between herself and Alex.

"Good morning, Tory," Justin said. "Want some coffee?"

"No, thanks. I'm going for a walk to clear my head."

"Want some company?" Alex asked. She got to her feet before Tory could answer.

Tory nodded. Both women got their coats and then walked into the chilly November morning. The snow from the night before blanketed the ground, and as she took in the scenery Tory realized how pure and innocent the world looked. A pleasant silence fell between them.

Then Alex spoke. "Okay, what's going on with you and my brother?"

Tory shrugged. Alex narrowed her eyes. "I'm not going to let this go."

"I'm not trying to keep you in the dark. I just don't know what's going on. I mean, I'm attracted to him, and he's funny and cute. But there's also a part of him that I'm not sure of." Tory knew she couldn't really say too much about Ben to Alex. She didn't know about his very serious side. The dangerous LASER operative who had saved her neck on Puerto Isla.

"Men complicate things endlessly."

"Does Justin do that for you?"

"Sometimes, but there are pluses to having him around."

"I bet," Tory said, smiling at her friend.

"He's also helping with the Rainy investigation."

"Because of his sister's death."

"Yes. Justin won't rest until he has all the facts."

"We won't, either," Tory said. "Did you have a chance to read the e-mail from Kayla?"

"Yes, what's up with Betsy?"

Betsy Stone was the nurse at Athena Academy. She'd been avoiding answering any questions about Rainy's supposed appendectomy.

"I'm not sure. It looks like she has something to hide."

"I know. I wish I knew where Sam was. Her e-mails are always so vague about her location." Samantha St. John, their CIA agent friend and the youngest Cassandra, communicated with them via sporadic e-mails.

"Well, she's on the trail of Rainy's killer."

"I wish we could find some concrete proof of what happened. Everything we've uncovered makes me very uncomfortable."

"Me, too. At least Darcy is safe now."

"Yes. Who would have guessed that Maurice Steele would be such a psycho? I'm glad I was able to help her nail that bastard."

"I wish I'd been in on it. It's situations like that one that the Cassandra promise was made for."

"I think Darcy didn't really want us to know how bad the situation with Maurice was."

"We can all be taken in by appearances sometimes."

"When you are in a situation like that, it's not always easy to be rational. And she wanted to protect her son at all costs."

"Well, don't you forget about the Cassandra promise. If you get in hot water, call for help."

"I will."

The women finished their walk and headed back to the house. Tory realized that she wasn't as alone as she'd thought she was. Maybe the reason that all of her close friends were from her Athena Academy days were due to the fact that she'd made the kind of bonds with them that weren't easily forged elsewhere.

When they got back to the house, they joined the rest of the family and Justin in Charles's den. Ben brought everyone up to speed on Tory's investigation. Tory used Charles's computer to search one of the many databases she had access to through the network system. Ben towered over her. Leaning against the desk, he watched every detail she came up with, but he was strangely quiet this morning.

Alex and Justin helped out and ran the names of all of Tory's subjects through the FBI database that they both had access to. Charles and Veronica drifted in and out of the room. Charles said it reminded him of the old days when he'd been active at the CIA. Veronica had worn a tired smile and said only that it reminded her of Alex and Ben's dad.

Her eyes had gotten teary and Ben had gone from the room with his mother. Alex and Justin followed them out, and soon Tory was alone.

Tory finally found a connection between Del Torro, Whitlow and Pearson. They'd all attended Oxford in England at the same time. "Pay dirt."

"What did you find?"

Tory glanced up. Ben stood in the doorway, his

shoulder nearly spanning the opening. "How's your mom?"

"She's fine. She always misses Dad at the holidays."

"What about you?"

He shrugged his shoulders. "I'm okay. What'd you find out?"

Tory didn't want to let the subject of his father go. But she was pursuing a story, and Ben was reluctant to talk about it. "Whitlow and Pearson were at Oxford with Del Torro."

"Nice connection, but still weak."

"I'm working on it."

"Tory, this package just arrived from your network," Alex said. She brought in a padded envelope that Tory knew contained the footage she'd requested of Pearson and Whitlow.

"Thanks."

Ben took the package and opened it up. Tory grabbed her notepad and moved to the love seat. Alex sat down next to her and wrapped an arm around her Tory's shoulder. "I'm glad you're here."

Tory hugged her friend back. "Me, too."

Alex left the room and Ben tossed her the remote and then joined her on the love seat. "What are we looking for?"

"I don't know. I ordered these so that I could see the way he moved and talked and maybe get a feeling for how to approach him."

The interview footage showed a man who was

smooth, suave and urbane. A man who moved through life as if he owned it. She learned he loved his yacht, the *Cleo,* and entertained both heads of state and celebrities on it.

She wondered if it was the same boat that both Addler and Terrence had fished with him on. She'd gone over the footage she'd shot in Addler's home, but the name of the boat hadn't been visible in the picture in Addler's office.

Veronica had secured an invitation for Ben and Tory to attend a party that evening that the Pearsons would be attending. Tory was more than a little nervous.

"I wish there was some way to tie Del Torro to the campaign."

"Have you searched the list?"

Tory rolled her eyes. "It was one of the first things I did."

"Let me see it."

She tossed him the three-inch-thick sheaf of papers. Ben groaned but started shifting through the sheets. Tory turned the volume up as a Discovery Channel special came on the tape. "Chris Pearson is known for his political influence and entrepreneurial skills, but he also has one of the most extensive collections of Egyptian artifacts in the United States. Today our cameras will be the first to see the collection that he started during a college trip with friends from Oxford."

The footage shifted from the reporter, Brett Brown, a guy Tory had met a few times, to film of Pearson walking through the hallway of his mansion in Alexandria, Virginia, and into a large collection room. It was filled with sarcophagi and other Egyptian artifacts. Pearson talked about his collection for almost ten minutes.

"You are part of a Society for Egypt."

"Nothing that formal. My group is just a bunch of friends from my college days who all share an interest in ancient Egypt."

"What's your group called?"

"Nothing showy—we're just the Egyptian Society. We came up with the name when we were at Oxford studying ancient civilizations."

"Is Governor Whitlow a member?" Brown asked. This interview had been filmed almost six years earlier when Whitlow had been the governor of Illinois.

"Yes, he is."

Tory froze the frame and glanced at Ben. He stopped fanning the pages of the contributions list. Tory went back to the computer and found the list on there. She found that the Egyptian Society had made numerous contributions to Whitlow's campaign. Tory did a separate search on Pearson and found he'd contributed money on his own. Del Torro's name didn't appear on the list.

"Here's the lead I was hoping for."

"It's still not solid."

"I'm not going to have to use it for evidence in a court of law. If I play my cards right, Pearson will tell me what I don't know."

"What's your plan?"

"My plan is to let him overhear you and I talking at this party. To make it sound like we know more than we do and then see how he reacts."

Chapter 18

Tory had been to fancy parties before as a guest and as a reporter covering events, so she had no real reason to be nervous tonight. Veronica Forsythe had picked out Tory's dress, a sexy black Gaultier gown. The black sheath hugged her tight across the breasts and had a simple black strap over one shoulder. Veronica had warmed up to Tory over the past few days and had taken Tory under her wing. Alex had warned that her mother was eyeing Tory has a potential daughter-in-law, but Ben didn't seem to mind, so Tory didn't dwell on it.

The limo pulled to a stop and they all got out of the car. "I'll be the envy of every man in the room tonight."

Ben offered his arm to his mother, and the three of

them walked up the steps and into the Gallery of Ancient Art, where the party was being held.

"I love this place at the holidays," Veronica said.

"Mom, you love any place where there's a party."

"So does my son," she said, leaning up and kissing Ben's cheek.

Tory observed them, realizing that Ben and his mother had a really close bond. She hadn't expected it, because Alex had told hair-raising tales about her mother's obsession with keeping up their blue-blood society appearance. But Ben and Veronica both were graced with charm and the ability to put anyone at ease. Tory could easily see why Ben was able to fool the world into believing he was happy as a playboy who lived off his inheritance.

They left their coats at the coat check, and Ben braved the bar to get them all drinks. Soon Veronica saw some friends and left Tory and Ben.

"Have you seen him yet?" Ben asked when they were alone.

"No. It's crowded in here. We could have some difficulty finding him."

"Mom said he's usually on the dance floor at these things. He and his wife took lessons last year and are eager to impress their friends."

Tory took a sip of her drink and waited for Ben to suggest they go out on the dance floor and look for Pearson. Ben surveyed the crowd and smiled at several people he knew. Placing his hand on the small of Tory's back, he escorted her to a group of his friends. Tory made small talk until finally her patience gave out. She gave her glass and Ben's to a passing waiter.

"Shall we dance?" she asked with her on-air smile.

Ben excused them from the group and they walked toward the dance floor. "The man's supposed to ask, Athena grad."

"If only he's astute enough to realize the lady wants to dance."

Ben gave her a grin that made her melt. He was too sexy for his own good. And damn him, he knew it.

"I knew you wouldn't be able to resist taking charge."

She had the feeling he was laughing at her, but it wasn't a cruel laughter. "You're too tricky for your own good."

"Don't tell my mom."

Ben led her through the crowd and onto the dance floor. The band was playing standards and as Ben swept her into his arms, "These Foolish Things" by Bryan Ferry came on. Was that all she was going to have of Ben after this story aired and it was time to move on—a collection of memories? She shivered as Ben's hand rested above her buttocks in the low V of her cocktail dress. His hands were warm and smooth against her back, and he traced an idle pattern there as he moved them through the crowd.

He was an expert dancer. Tory let him completely control her body and searched the crowd for Pearson. They found him at the center of the floor, dancing with his wife.

Ben leaned down and brushed his lips over her cheek, stopping next to her ear. "Now what?"

Shivers of longing and desire flooded her.

"Tory?"

She rested her head on his shoulder and whispered against his neck, "Let him see us."

Ben nodded. He danced them closer to Pearson. Tory glanced at him, trying to be nonchalant, but when their gazes collided Pearson froze. Tory smiled and Ben danced them away from the Pearsons.

Lydia Pearson had the kind of height Tory had long envied. She was at least five foot seven, slender and had the kind of tan that came from a salon. Her sleek blond hair was pulled back, and her strapless gown gave her a look of ageless beauty.

Chris Pearson was dressed in a black dinner jacket. He was only a few inches taller than his wife and had thick blond hair. They moved together well.

"Did you see the way he looked at me?" Tory asked. She'd leaned up on tiptoe to speak into Ben's ear. Ben tightened his grip on her. For a moment she was completely surrounded by him.

"Yes. There he goes."

Ben took Tory's hand and pulled her through the crowd behind Pearson. They paused at the bar so that he didn't notice them following. He left his wife at their dinner table and headed up the stairs.

"You stay here and keep an eye on Mrs. Pearson. I'll follow him." Tory didn't want Ben to be put at risk of exposing his cover to Pearson or any of his acquaintances.

"Yeah, right," Ben said, taking her hand he led her up the stairs.

Tory pulled him to a stop in a quiet alcove. "I'm serious about this, Ben. If you go with me, he'll suspect you're something more than just a man who lives off his trust fund."

"Why? I could just be on a polite date with my little sister's friend. I'm not letting you go alone," he said with a finality that almost touched her.

"Ben—"

"Don't say you can protect yourself. I know you can. I have instincts, too, and they won't let me let you leave on your own."

"We're bound to get separated at some point."

"Take this," Ben said, pressing a small communication device into her hand.

"What is it?"

"It's a two-way tracker, cell phone and radio."

"Wow, I like your gadgets."

"I know you do," he said, leaning in for a fierce kiss.

"Here's how it works." He pushed a few buttons on the device, and the display screen became active. Two flashing dots, one gray and one green, appeared. Ben handed the phone to Tory and took two steps away from her. She watched the gray dot move.

"So now we'll each know where the other one is at all times," she said.

"Yes. If you get into trouble, push the star key and I'll come running."

"What if you get into trouble?"

"Tory, it's me."

That's what she was afraid of. Ben attracted trouble like a lawless bandit.

The second floor wasn't as crowded as the dance floor but it was still a crush. This level was filled with diorama displays of everyday life in ancient times. Tory moved past the most unlifelike figures she'd ever seen. Not only did they not look real, but they also looked a little creepy.

"What now?" Ben asked.

"Let's split up and work the crowd. I'll meet you on the other side."

Ben nodded and moved to the left. Tory worked her way slowly through the right side of the room. She didn't see Pearson but noticed that Dave Addler was at the party.

"Miss Patton, it's a pleasure to see you again."

Boy, you could tell the man had spent too much time in the diplomatic corps, because he lied with real sincerity.

"You, too. Is your wife with you tonight? I wanted to talk to her about Puerto Isla."

"No, she's spending the holidays in France with her family. I'm leaving in the morning to join her. Did you make any headway with the story you were pursuing?"

"It's coming along nicely."

He excused himself and Tory moved on. She wasn't sure about Addler. She wanted to get Ben's opinion. Ben was waiting at the bar when she finally made it across the room. He handed her an amaretto sour. Tory took a sip but didn't want to drink tonight, so she set the glass on the bar and asked for some water.

"Anything?" she asked Ben when the bartender had moved away.

"Nothing. You?"

"I ran into Dave Addler. He was friendly."

"The man's a diplomat, Tory. That's really not suspicious behavior."

"I know. I'm not sure what to make of his involvement. He's a wild card."

"What do we do now?"

Tory shrugged. She was out of ideas. If Pearson wasn't around, they were going to have a hard time letting him eavesdrop and learn that they had proof he'd used drug money to fund Whitlow's campaign.

"I wish I had a cameraman with me. Then I could just point my microphone and start asking questions."

Ben gave her a quick hug. "Don't sound so forlorn."

"There he is," Tory said. Pearson was coming closer.

"Where?" Ben asked.

"Don't look. I think he spotted us." She took Ben's hand and pulled him to an area where the crowds were thinner. She stopped to see if Pearson followed them. She leaned up and whispered to Ben. "He's getting close. Time to put our plan in action."

Ben wrapped his arm around her shoulders and pulled her into a spot between the display areas. The lighting was dim. This was the perfect place for lovers to stop for a few quiet moments.

"Do you think he knows you're on to him?" Ben asked.

"Probably, but it doesn't matter. I have hard proof that he funneled drug money into Whitlow's campaign. When I air my story tomorrow, it'll all be over for him."

"It's lucky you saw him on Puerto Isla," Ben said.

"Yes, it is. I wouldn't have known to look at Oxford otherwise."

Tory didn't have much more than the Oxford connection, and Ben knew it. He put his arm around her waist. "I'll be glad when this story is over so you'll have more time for me."

Though they'd planned a quiet interlude so that Pearson wouldn't suspect they'd set him up, Tory hadn't expected the words Ben had just said. "I'm always going to be busy."

"Maybe I can convince you to free up a little more time." Ben's head dipped and he cupped her face in his large hands. His mouth took hers with languid sweeps of his tongue. She lifted her hands to his shoulders then higher, pushing her fingers into his thick hair and holding him to her.

She didn't know if he was still playing a part or if he really wanted more of her time. She didn't want to think about Ben and the complications that were implicit in even contemplating a relationship with him. He'd claimed her as his own. He was her lover and her partner in this dangerous game, but at the same time, she still wasn't confident he'd be around after Christmas.

Tory slipped her arm through Ben's and they finished walking through the exhibit. Ben leaned down to kiss her. "Do you think he heard us?"

"We'll have to wait and see what he does."

"You live an odd life, Miss Patton."

"You should talk."

"It was an observation, not an accusation."

They went back downstairs in time for dinner to be served. Veronica was waiting for them at the table.

"There you two are. Having fun?"

"Always," Ben said. He held out his mother's chair and then turned to seat Tory. The other people at their table for eight were all friends of Veronica.

Dinner was a slow affair, and when it was over Ben excused himself. Everyone at the table was engrossed in their conversations, and Veronica leaned close to Tory.

"I think Ben's serious about you."

Tory had no idea what to say. "Don't—"

"Let me finish, dear. I know he seems as if he drifts through life and lets nothing touch him. But he's fiercely loyal to those he loves and will do everything in his power to keep them safe."

"I know."

"I won't tolerate anyone using him," Veronica said quietly.

"I'm not. I care for your son."

Veronica nodded. "Good. I like you, Tory Patton."

Tory's cell phone rang and she turned away from Veronica to answer it. "Patton here."

"Miss Patton, this is Chris Pearson."

"What can I do for you?"

"I have captured your lover and will kill him unless you surrender the proof you have against me."

Tory's heart stopped beating for a second, and blood rushed in her ears. Of all the possible outcomes she'd projected, Ben being captured hadn't been one of them. She was afraid for Ben and knew she could accomplish nothing if she didn't stay focused. She pushed her own emotions away and hoped she could keep them bottled until she was able to save Ben. "Where are you?"

"That's not important. Meet me at midnight on the mall by the carousel."

"Okay," she said, trying to sound casual so she didn't alarm Veronica. And so that Pearson wouldn't suspect how angry and scared she really was.

"Come alone and bring all the evidence you've accumulated."

"I can't gather it all that quickly."

"For Ben's sake I hope you can."

Tory's heart leaped and she realized she'd miscalculated when she'd set up her plan. She'd forgotten to take into account that trapped wolves were willing to do anything to survive.

"I've got to go," she said to Veronica.

"Is everything okay?" Veronica asked.

Tory wasn't sure how to tell the other woman that thanks to her bluffing Ben had been captured by a crazy man. Though she didn't really think Pearson was crazy, just desperate.

"Everything's fine. I got a lead on the story I've been working on."

"I'll give your regrets to Ben."

"He's meeting me out front."

"You can take the limo if you need to."

"Thank you, Veronica. But we'll use a cab."

"I enjoyed spending the evening with you, Tory. I hope we'll be seeing more of you with Ben."

Tory sincerely hoped so, too. "I've got to run."

Tory left without a backward glance. If Ben was harmed because of her, she was going to go ballistic on Chris Pearson. She'd lay waste to more than his reputation in a jury of public opinion. She'd completely ruin the man.

In the lobby Tory reached into her purse and pulled out the phone Ben had given her. The phone gave her the exact coordinates of Ben's location, and Tory wasted no time leaving the party to rescue him. She retrieved her coat and Ben's from the coatroom so that Veronica wouldn't be suspicious.

She and Ben had stowed their luggage in the limo.

In the back of the car Tory quickly changed from her party dress into a pair of dark slacks, a sweater and her leather jacket. Ben had no weapons in his suitcase, and all Tory had was her hunting knife. She slipped it into the ankle sheath and climbed out of the car.

Tory hailed a cab and gave him directions, praying the entire time that Ben was still alive.

Chapter 19

Tory had the cab let her off a block from Ben's coordinates. She was in the Crystal City area near the Pentagon by a row of darkened office buildings. The streets were almost empty. An occasional car drove by, but there were no pedestrians save her on this cold November evening.

Blending with the shadows, she carefully approached Ben's location. She stood in front of the five-story office building. She checked the time on her watch. It was ten-thirty, almost an hour since Pearson's call.

There were two cars parked in the adjacent lot, and Tory decided she'd check out the building. If she couldn't get inside she'd wait until they brought Ben out to meet her and attack then.

Tory went around the back to the loading dock and checked the door. She'd done a story nine months ago on electronic security systems. Eighty percent of all residences and businesses only paid to have the front of the building wired. Tory checked the back door and found that this building fell in that eighty percent.

Tory took a nail file from her purse and a bobby pin from her hair and picked the lock. She stowed the items and stepped inside the building. It was quiet and Tory glanced at the phone display screen one more time. She and Ben should be on top of each other according to this. She searched for the stairwell and found it. Quickly she climbed to the second floor and searched it.

Empty.

The third floor was the same. Empty offices only. But on the fourth floor she heard the murmur of voices as she quietly opened the door from the stairwell.

Was Pearson here with an accomplice? Or was he only talking to Ben? Tory wasted no time, slipping silently toward the voices.

Light spilled from the room. Tory moved closer to the wall, careful to stay to the shadows.

She paused outside the door, then took out her compact and angled it so she could see into the room without revealing herself. There were two men in the room. Pearson faced the doorway; the other man had his back toward her. Tory couldn't identify him. Where was Ben?

"You're an idiot. We can't kill a Forsythe without raising suspicion. The pilot no one cares about, but this guy…"

Pearson stared at the man in front of him. "They have enough evidence to incriminate me."

"What kind?" the first man asked. His voice was familiar, but Tory couldn't place it. They were speaking in low tones, almost whispering.

"I don't know. Forsythe passed out when I hit him. I told Patton to bring it to me," Pearson said.

Tory didn't believe that Ben had passed out. It would take more than a punch from Pearson to bring him down. Ben was waiting for the right moment. Tory knew she just had to give it to him and together they could take the two men.

"Do you honestly think she'll show up alone? She'll probably be there with her camera crew and show your face on live TV."

From her limited view of both men in the mirror, she couldn't see any weapons. But surely if they'd captured Ben they were armed.

"It's too late. I'm not letting either of them walk away alive."

"It was too late from the moment King surfaced alive."

Tory dropped to the floor and peeked into the room. It was a standard office with bookcases on one wall and two leather wing-back chairs with a small coffee table between them.

The only light came from the desk lamp, which left the area around the door not well lit. The office wasn't that big but it was clearly an executive one. There were some potted plants in one corner and a puddle of darkness in the area around it. Tory crept into the room on her hands and knees. She froze when she realized that Pearson had a gun trained on him. And that the man holding him hostage was Dave Addler.

"Killing me isn't going to save you, Dave. She knows everything."

"How can she? We have the only real proof."

Ben lay bound and gagged next to Pearson's chair. He opened his eyes and glanced sharply at Tory. She had no idea what he was trying to communicate, but she was very happy to see he was alive. She took the knife from her boot and slid it to Ben across the carpeted floor. He fumbled until he caught the handle and closed his eyes again.

"She knows about Oxford and the contributions through the society."

"I'll modify the membership list. And take Alejandro Del Torro's name off."

"I don't think that will work."

"You haven't been thinking straight for a while. When are you meeting with Patton?"

"Midnight."

"What are you planning to do with Forsythe's body?"

"Drop him in the Potomac. This time with better weights."

Tory crawled back out of the room and got to her feet. They always said that in life-and-death situations instinct took over. She really wished she'd had been in a dojo in the past few months so her tae kwon do skills weren't as rusty. She closed her eyes and asked Rainy to help her out.

"I don't think that's a good plan," Tory said from the doorway. Addler fired in her direction, and the bullet went a little wide, hitting the door frame and not her.

She really hated being shot at. She gathered herself and ran toward Addler, hitting his shoulder with a flying side kick.

He stumbled backward, firing at her, but his shot was wide and missed her. Pearson was screaming something but Tory couldn't make out his words. She focused instead on Addler and getting the gun away from him.

Pearson got to his feet at the same moment that Ben sat up and cut the bonds to his feet. Ben flung the knife at Pearson, catching him in the arm.

Ben battled Pearson, but Tory focused on Addler, who was determined to kill her. Addler fired again. Tory ducked but felt the bullet graze her arm. She attacked Addler again, hitting him hard on the chest. He stumbled backward, falling to his knees but not releasing the gun.

He fired a third time. This time the bullet ripped through Tory's thigh and she screamed. She lashed out with a front snap kick, catching him under the chin and snapping his head back. She followed it up with a downward heel strike to the nose. Blood splurted everywhere. Tory reached for his gun hand, wrestling the weapon from him.

Ben took the gun from Tory. "I've got this."

Ben was bruised and bloodied. She touched his face, wiping a smear of blood from his lips. "Oh, Ben."

Tory was painfully aware that filing the story of a lifetime paled next to the fear she'd felt when she thought Ben was dead. Or the emotions that were flooding through her now. Coming so close to losing Ben made her realize how much she wanted him in her life—for good.

Robert O'Neill and several other men she recognized from Puerto Isla as being on Ben's team entered the room and took control of the situation. Tory wondered how they'd known where to come, but before she could ask spots danced in front of her eyes and she collapsed.

She woke in Ben's arms. Two paramedics hovered nearby. They had bandaged her arm and her thigh. "I need to get to the studio to cover this story."

"Tory, let it go."

"I can't. This is my exclusive. Am I okay?" she asked the paramedic.

"You're shocky, so you should take it easy for the next few days," he said.

"I'm just talking about sitting at a news desk and reading a TelePrompter," Tory said.

"Yes, but only if you take a week off after that," the paramedic said.

"She will," Ben said.

"I've got to go," she said, and forcing herself to her feet, she limped out of the room.

It was almost 9:00 a.m. the next morning when Tory exited of the UBC studios in Washington, D.C. She was exhausted, but knew she wouldn't sleep tonight. Tyson Bedders had been over the moon when Tory had talked to him.

They'd aired her live story of political corruption. She'd started with Whitlow, Del Torro and Pearson and how the men had met at Oxford in their college years. Pearson had tried to justify his actions by saying that Alejandro Del Torro had needed U.S. funding to make the lives of the people of Puerto Isla easier. But in the end that hadn't mattered. King's team had unknowingly witnessed Pearson on the island, funding the rebel movement that was responsible for the coup that ousted Santiago.

The White House press secretary had quickly issued a statement that James Whitlow had no idea that Pearson had been channeling illegal drug money into his campaign fund. He promised to start his own investigation and rectify the matter.

Pearson and Addler had both been arrested for their connection to the Jimenez murder. Tory and Ben had both witnessed their confession.

Whitlow had also agreed to do an interview with Tory in the coming month. That interview would be used to launch Tory's new spot on UBC's biweekly newsmagazine, *A Closer Look.* Tory had everything she'd ever dreamed of.

Almost.

"Need a ride?"

Ben stood in the entryway to the studios, his heavy overcoat dusted with the light snow that was falling. He looked tired, but otherwise she couldn't read any emotion on his face. He wasn't the charming Society Sam at this moment, nor the LASER operative.

"Thanks."

Ben slipped his arm around her shoulder and led her to his car. He opened the passenger door for her, but before she could climb into the car, he took her in his arms. "Dammit, you scared me last night."

She held him as tightly as he held her. "You're not the only one. How does someone with your kind of training get kidnapped?"

"Hey, I had to take a leak."

Tory closed her eyes and just breathed in the scent of him, thankful that he was still here with her and that she was in his strong arms.

"You saved my ass," he said.

She slid her hands down his back and cupped his backside. "It's worth saving."

She didn't want to let this get too serious. She didn't trust what she felt for Ben.

"I'm not kidding, Tory."

"I know. Every time I close my eyes, I see you lying bound on the floor again and this time you don't get up."

He made a rough sound deep in his throat and then lifted her face to his, kissing her deeply and holding her to him with a strength that would have frightened her a few weeks ago. But now it felt right that he should need her as desperately as she desired him.

"Come home with me. Let me make love to you so that I can forget that moment when Addler shot his gun at you and I heard you scream."

Tory nodded. Ben hustled her into the car and drove them quickly to his apartment. He started kissing her in the elevator, his hands roaming up and down her body, being careful of her gunshot wounds. She did the same to him, understanding that these caresses were for both of them a way of confirming that the other was alive and well.

Ben lifted her into his arms when the elevator stopped on his floor. He had the door open in no time flat. He slammed it closed behind them and walked her into his bedroom before laying her gently on the bed.

He unfastened her bra and tenderly palmed her breasts in both hands. His mouth slid along her neck and caressed her lightly at the base. She shivered, undulating against him. She grabbed his shoulders and encountered his heavy topcoat. She pushed at the fabric, finally forcing it off his shoulders. His hands left her breasts for a minute, and he tossed his coat aside and then ripped off his shirt.

"Tell me if I hurt you," he said.

In response she stroked the rippling muscles of his chest, tugging on the light patch of hair and scraping her fingernail over his flat nipples. He groaned her name and lifted her with his hands under her armpits.

"Open your legs."

She did and he moved between them, still being careful of the bandages. His mouth fastened on one of her nipples, suckling her. She tilted her head back. His hands slid between their bodies, unfastening her pants and then slipping between her skin and her clothing. Delving deeply into the moist center of her body.

He lifted her feet and pushed her pants to the floor. Ben unfastened his own pants and freed his erection. He lifted her again and she wrapped her legs around his waist. He turned to rest her weight on his body. She pulled his head to hers and thrust her tongue deep into his mouth as he entered her.

She moved over him, setting a rhythm that took them both rapidly toward their climaxes. Ben's hands roamed over her back, and then as she tightened and tried to move faster, he gripped her buttocks and held her still. Then he thrust up into her once, twice and finally a third time, pushing her over the edge. She held tightly to him as she cried his name. He thrust into her one more time before his own shout of completion echoed in the quiet apartment.

* * *

One week later, Tory was back in Manhattan. Ben had gotten a call in the middle of the night and left her alone at his place. Finally she had returned to her city, her apartment and her successful career. Ben's picture had appeared in Britain's leading paper. He'd had his arm around two ladies and the caption had claimed he was in town to celebrate the holiday season in style.

Tory knew that Ben wasn't involved with either of the women—probably hadn't even been there—but she also didn't know where in the world he was. And she was worried about him.

She'd gone back to checking into Rainy's death, searching databases for any additional clues about the fertility clinic burglary or anything at all that might be a lead to Rainy's killer or her child. She and the other Cassandras were in touch constantly, but so far nothing more had been found.

There was some lingering public sentiment that the Athena Academy did more harm than good to the young women who attended the school, and Tory was planning a series of in-depth interviews with current students, as well as alumnae to show just how beneficial the school was.

She'd also been in contact with AA.gov. They'd found the woman who'd leaked information. She was one of Dave Addler's aides. Apparently once Chris Pearson had mentioned that Tory was on Puerto Isla,

Addler had used his diplomatic connections to find out information on Tory.

When her name came up in the AA.gov system, Addler had used it to try to discourage Tory from pursuing the story. They'd taken care of the problem, but weren't going to be able to use her anymore.

Tory didn't mind. She'd found enough excitement without being a government courier. She was going to be the next Diane Sawyer.

She'd gone to Florida for two days and visited her parents and her brother and his family. Derrick was recovering nicely and didn't hold her responsible for his injuries. Pearson had rolled over on Addler big time and had given the investigators the names of every person that Addler had tried to eliminate from the picture, including her brother. Her parents had smothered her in love, and she'd come back to New York refreshed. In fact, the only thing left open in her life was Ben.

Was he going to call her?

A knock sounded on her door. "Come in."

It was Perry. She was surprised to see him. He'd avoided her since she'd been back in the office.

"Got a minute?"

"Not really. What do you want?"

"To apologize. I realize it's too little too late, but I didn't mean to hurt you."

"What's this really about?" Tory asked.

"Nothing. I cared for you. I don't want to leave things the way they ended at my apartment."

"Apology accepted. Please leave."

He paused in the doorway. "I'd like to produce some of the work you're doing for *A Closer Look*."

Perry was a good producer and in the end she couldn't hold their failed relationship against him. Though it did hurt that the woman he'd taken up with was Shannon Conner. "I'll think about it."

He nodded and then left quietly. Tory folded her arms together and lowered her head to them. She hadn't loved Perry and wasn't really mad at him any longer. But what did it say about her that she'd been involved with him for four years? Was she incapable of the kind of depth of feelings that were needed for a real relationship?

She left the office just before five and headed home. She ordered takeout from her favorite Italian place and toasted her new success by herself in her apartment with a bottle of Merlot. She curled up on her sofa and put *Top Gun* in the DVD player.

The doorbell rang while Maverick and Goose were playing volleyball against Iceman. She paused the movie and went to the door.

"Who is it?"

"Ben."

She opened the door. He was leaner than the last time she'd seen him, and beard stubble covered his jaw.

"Sorry I didn't call."

"That's okay. I figured you couldn't."

"Can I come in?"

She realized she was blocking the door. She stepped back and he entered. He dropped a flight bag on the floor and glanced around her apartment.

"Planning to stay?"

"As long as you'll have me."

"This is complicated."

"You have no idea. But dammit, I missed you."

"I missed you, too."

He opened his arms and she stepped into them. "I know you're not ready for commitment and I'm willing to let you set the pace for a while. But I'm not letting you go."

"Good. And maybe I am ready for commitment. With the right guy."

"Me?"

"Yeah, you."

His smile made her heart beat faster. He scooped her up in his arms and carried her to the sofa. She made love to him and then pampered her warrior home from the battle.

Their relationship was going to have to be taken slowly because of the dedication and travel that their careers demanded. But when she took him to her bed, Tory knew she'd finally found a man she could have a future with. A man who was her equal and not threatened by her. And an Athena woman would settle for nothing less.

* * *

Don't miss Double-Cross, *available next month.*

▼ SILHOUETTE®
Sensation™

DEADLY EXPOSURE
by Linda Turner

Turning Points

A picture is worth a thousand words, but the killer Lily Fitzgerald had unknowingly photographed only used four: *You're going to die.* Lily didn't want to depend on anyone for help – especially not pulse-stopping, green-eyed cop Tony Giovani. But now her only protection from the man who threatened her life was the man who threatened her heart.

ALSO AVAILABLE NEXT MONTH

DOUBLE-CROSS by Meredith Fletcher
Bombshell: Athena Force

RUNNING SCARED by Linda Winstead Jones
Last Chance Heroes

DANGEROUS GAMES by Marie Ferrarella
Cavanaugh Justice

HEIR TO DANGER by Valerie Parv
Code of the Outback

GUARDING LAURA by Susan Vaughan

Don't miss out! On sale 15th July 2005

Visit our website at www.silhouette.co.uk

Available at most branches of WHSmith, Tesco, ASDA, Martins, Borders, Eason, Sainsbury's and most good paperback bookshops.

SILHOUETTE BOMBSHELL

Your opinion is important to us!

The novel you have just read is a *Bombshell* book. This mini-series features high stakes suspense and action-adventure stories in which the heroine saves the day. Filled with twists and turns, these books are unpredictable, fast-paced reads with an element of romance.

Please take a few minutes to share your thoughts with us about Bombshell books. Your comments will ensure that we continue to deliver fiction that you love to read.

1. Where did you buy this book?

    From a supermarket ❑   Through our Reader Service™ ❑
    From a bookshop ❑   Other (please state) ❑
    On the Internet ❑   _____

2. Which of the following best describes how likely you would be to buy a Bombshell book in the next 12 months?

    Definitely would buy ❑   Probably would not buy ❑
    Probably would buy ❑   Definitely would not buy ❑
    Might or might not buy ❑   _____

3. Could Bombshell become a regular purchase for you in the future?

    Yes ❑   No ❑

4.a) Overall, how would you rate the reading experience of Bombshell books?

    Excellent ❑   Fair ❑
    Very good ❑   Poor ❑
    Good ❑

4.b) Why do you say that? Please describe your experience in more detail below.

_____

_____

_____

_____

5. Please indicate the most important factor that made you buy this book.

The picture on the cover ❑   I enjoy the Sensation series ❑
The author ❑   The description on the back cover ❑
The title ❑   I borrowed/was given this book ❑
Other (please state) _____

6. In the Bombshell books you have read, how do *you* feel about the level of...

	too much	too little	just right
Romance in the books	❑	❑	❑
Action-adventure in the books	❑	❑	❑
Suspense in the books	❑	❑	❑
Unpredictability in the books	❑	❑	❑

7. For each of the Mills & Boon® and Silhouette® series, please tick all series that you currently read.

Mills & Boon Modern Romance™ ❑
Mills & Boon Tender Romance™ ❑
Mills & Boon Medical Romance™ ❑
Mills & Boon Sensual Romance™ ❑
Mills & Boon Historical Romance™ ❑
Mills & Boon Blaze™ ❑
Silhouette Desire™ ❑
Silhouette Special Edition™ ❑
Silhouette Sensation™ ❑
Silhouette Intrigue™ ❑
Silhouette Superromance™ ❑

9. Which age bracket do you belong to? Your answers will remain confidential.

16-24 ❑   25-34 ❑   35-49 ❑
50-64 ❑   65+ ❑

This completes the survey.
Thank you for taking the time to tell us what you think!
Please send your completed questionnaire to the address below:

READER SURVEY, PO Box 676, Richmond, Surrey, TW9 1WU.

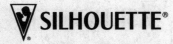 **SILHOUETTE**®

is proud to present an exciting new series from
international bestselling author

MARIE FERRARELLA

Don't miss the thrilling

A family that fight for what's right—and their reward is lasting love.

4 FREE

BOOKS AND A SURPRISE GIFT!

We would like to take this opportunity to thank you for reading this Silhouette® book by offering you the chance to take FOUR more specially selected titles from the Sensation™ series absolutely FREE! We're also making this offer to introduce you to the benefits of the Reader Service™—

- ★ FREE home delivery
- ★ FREE gifts and competitions
- ★ FREE monthly Newsletter
- ★ Exclusive Reader Service offers
- ★ Books available before they're in the shops

Accepting these FREE books and gift places you under no obligation to buy, you may cancel at any time, even after receiving your free shipment. Simply complete your details below and return the entire page to the address below. You don't even need a stamp!

YES! Please send me 4 free Sensation books and a surprise gift. I understand that unless you hear from me, I will receive 6 superb new titles every month for just £3.05 each, postage and packing free. I am under no obligation to purchase any books and may cancel my subscription at any time. The free books and gift will be mine to keep in any case.

S5ZED

Ms/Mrs/Miss/Mr ....Initials ....

BLOCK CAPITALS PLEASE

Surname ....

Address ....

....

....Postcode..............................

Send this whole page to:
UK: FREEPOST CN81, Croydon, CR9 3WZ